"Be a good sold question me, C stay alive."

She nodded, appreciating the strength in Griffin's blue eyes. Her life had been blasted apart and the only thing she had left was this man, this violent stranger.

Who'd just promised her she'd be okay.

"From the angle of the shot that was just fired," he said, "I figure the shooter is out back with a clear view of the living room. Stay low. When you hear me fire, race to the car and wait for me."

She nodded, her pulse pounding in her ears.

And then he kissed her, a brief touch of their lips.

"Good luck," he said.

It felt more like goodbye.

PAT
WHITE

UNDERCOVER
STRANGER

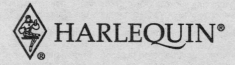

TORONTO • NEW YORK • LONDON
AMSTERDAM • PARIS • SYDNEY • HAMBURG
STOCKHOLM • ATHENS • TOKYO • MILAN • MADRID
PRAGUE • WARSAW • BUDAPEST • AUCKLAND

To amazing storyteller Mary Buckham
for the tour of The Fort, brainstorming and friendship.

Recycling programs
for this product may
not exist in your area.

ISBN-13: 978-0-373-69380-1
ISBN-10:   0-373-69380-X

UNDERCOVER STRANGER

Copyright © 2009 by Pat White

www.eHarlequin.com

Printed in U.S.A.

ABOUT THE AUTHOR

Growing up in the Midwest, Pat White has been spinning stories in her head ever since she was a little girl—stories filled with mystery, romance and adventure. Years later, while trying to solve the mysteries of raising a family in a house full of men, she started writing romance fiction. After six Golden Heart nominations and a *Romantic Times BOOKreviews* Award for Best Contemporary Romance (2004), her passion for storytelling and love of a good romance continues to find a voice in her tales of romantic suspense. Pat now lives in the Pacific Northwest and she's still trying to solve the mysteries of living in a house full of men—with the added complication of two silly dogs and three spoiled cats. She loves to hear from readers, so please visit her at www.patwhitebooks.com.

Books by Pat White

HARLEQUIN INTRIGUE

944—SILENT MEMORIES
968—THE AMERICAN TEMP AND THE BRITISH INSPECTOR*
974—THE ENGLISH DETECTIVE AND THE ROOKIE AGENT*
980—MISS FAIRMONT AND THE GENTLEMAN INVESTIGATOR*
1038—SOLDIER SURRENDER
1058—LOVING THE ENEMY
1113—UNDERCOVER STRANGER†

*The Blackwell Group
†Assignment: The Girl Next Door

CAST OF CHARACTERS

Griffin Black—Senior agent for AW-21, Griff's assignment is to trace a microchip created by terrorists to control jet engines.

Ciara O'Malley—She took over her grandmother Ruth's, doll museum when Ruth died. Ciara doesn't realize that dolls are being used for smuggling.

Adele—Ruth's best friend and surrogate mom to Ciara.

Dalton Keen—AW-21 agent ready to serve as back-up in case things go wrong.

Officer Banks—Police officer with questionable motives who helps Ciara after she's mugged.

AW-21—Covert branch of the National Security Agency designed to defend the United States against terrorism.

Chapter One

Her eyes enchanted him.

Crystal clear, blue with a hint of silver. Griffin Black studied the doll, set behind the protective glass, and hoped she wasn't the one he'd have to carve into pieces to accomplish his mission.

Pressing the two-inch digital reader to the glass, he waited to see if it registered integrated circuit activity. So far he'd struck out with most of the dolls on display. The D.R. read negative on the black-haired beauty, as well.

He glanced at the remaining dolls left to scan in the Seattle suburban museum, trying to determine which was the perfect one in which to hide the microchip. The bastards had been clever to use such an innocent vehicle to transport their contraband. They were determined to wreak havoc on their enemy: Americans.

"Can I help you?" a female voice said.

Griff slipped the reader into his pocket and turned to the source of the question, a petite woman with shoulder-length, striking red hair and emerald green eyes. She looked like she belonged behind glass.

"No." He paused. "Thank you."

He'd been so absorbed by the dolls that he hadn't sensed her approach. Lately he wondered if he was losing his edge.

"Do you have any questions?" she asked.

What she probably wanted to know was what a guy like Griff was doing in a doll museum.

"Where did they all come from?" A fairly innocuous question, he hoped. He didn't want to draw attention to himself. Then again, he couldn't be more out of place surrounded by the delicate creatures on display.

"Our dolls come from all over the world," she said with excitement in her voice. "Some we purchase and some are donated. Collectors are passionate about their dolls and want to make sure their passion lives on after they're gone."

She glanced at Griff with those beautiful emerald eyes, perfect enough to be a doll's. He must have been staring because she blinked and glanced at a Native American doll in the next case.

"My daughter collects dolls," he offered as an excuse for being here. There was no daughter. "I'm in town on business and thought I might pick her up something."

"How old is she?"

"Ten," he answered. Well, he *might* have had a ten-year-old daughter if he and Mary had stayed together. His engagement was one of the many casualties of the job.

"Ten is a nice age." She glanced at the blue-eyed doll in the case as if drifting back to her own childhood.

The nostalgic look in her eyes made him uncomfortable. He couldn't remember anything before his tour in Bosnia.

"We have a gift shop downstairs," she offered. "Stop

in before you leave. I'm sure we can find the perfect gift for her."

"I'll do that, thanks. Are you the curator?" he asked.

"I'm the owner, actually."

A shame. He hoped he'd happened upon an innocent, maybe even someone who could help him identify the criminals involved in this conspiracy. Instead he was looking into the eyes of a deceitful, but beautiful, spy. Recent Intel indicated that the smuggling activities had continued after Ruth O'Malley's death, which meant she must have passed down the responsibility to this woman. Her granddaughter?

"I'm Ciara O'Malley."

She extended her hand and he shook it, aware of how delicate it felt in his.

"Griffin Black."

"Nice to meet you."

He held on to her hand for a second longer than necessary. Her cheeks flushed, and with a nervous smile she snatched back her hand.

"I heard about your place from my aunt," he said. "She was friends with Ruth. Your grandmother, I'm assuming?"

Her face brightened, and she nodded. "Who's your aunt?"

"Miriam Anderson."

"I remember Mrs. Anderson. Nice lady with the fourteen cats. How's she doing in Phoenix?"

This is where Griff hoped his people had done their jobs.

"Not well, I'm afraid. She's had some health issues. She was sorry to hear about Ruth's passing. Sudden, was it?"

"Yes, sort of. She got pneumonia and everyone thought she'd make it, but she didn't."

But she could have. Griff wondered if her death had anything to do with her extracurricular activities. Did she screw up one too many shipments? Or betray a buyer?

"I'm sorry," he said.

She glanced at him. "Thanks. It's been hard, but each day gets a little better. Well, I'll be downstairs working and stuff." She smiled and disappeared around the corner.

Griff sensed her apprehension around him. Good, he would use that to keep her off balance.

At that moment he knew that if she weren't his enemy, she'd make the perfect mark. Either way he needed her in order to complete this mission, find the microchip and destroy it before the terrorists put it to use.

He'd start by completing a more extensive background check on Ciara, find out where she lived, what kind of coffee she drank, what she did for fun. He had some thoughts of his own on that subject.

"Not with this one," he muttered.

She was a mark and a spy, not a plaything, not a fellow agent who could use some meaningless sex to release the inner demons. No, Ciara was more important than that.

Important, but in the end, disposable.

They all were. Even Griff, he reminded himself. The minute he was no longer useful to AW-21, a covert branch of the National Security Administration, they'd red-tag him, or worse: ship him out to some isolated part of the world like they had done to Dalton Keen. AW-21 had sent Keen to a remote spot on the Olympic Peninsula to contemplate the error in judgment that nearly got him and a hostage killed. Good thing Griff had been able to rescue the kid from terrorist hell. Dalton Keen was a decent agent who'd made a bad call by trusting the wrong person.

Since *trust* wasn't in Griff's vocabulary, he would never make that mistake.

He wandered to the next display case to consider the remaining possibilities for smuggling the microchip. The plaque at the base of the glass read: *Dolls are a reflection of our humanity.*

He eyed the bride and groom dolls, the man dressed in a black tuxedo and his bride in a white gown holding a bouquet of red roses. Their expressions were peaceful, blissful. Was that supposed to be a reflection of humanity? Nah, just a fantasy, Griff thought, remembering the day he realized his commitment to fighting terrorism and avenging his sister Beth's death would prevent him from living a normal life.

The image of Mary lying in a hospital bed filled his thoughts. That was the reflection of his humanity: violence. Knowing she deserved better and fearing he was the cause of her accident, Griff, who she knew as Nicholas Drake, planned his own death. Three months later, Nicholas Drake officially died in a car crash and Griffin Black, a man with no ties to another living soul, was born.

His buddy, Carter, also an AW-21 agent, accused Griff of being cruel to the love of his life. Was it cruel to want to protect Mary from the ugliness of his world? The same type of ugliness that took his sister's life on 9/11?

Hell, he was in a dark place today, he realized, moving on to the next display case. Shaking it off, he focused on his mission. Pulling out a small notebook, he jotted notes about the dolls' origins, who donated them and when.

Ambling to the next display, he couldn't help but think about the redhead, so pleasant and innocent. Yet she'd been unable to maintain eye contact, indicating she wasn't comfortable chatting with him. He sensed she didn't have a lot of experience with men.

Griff stopped in front of the next display case and studied the doll, a young Japanese warrior who led a rebel army to defend his religious beliefs.

At least the kid was fighting for something honorable.

Griff's work had been honorable at the beginning, but somehow over the past few years it had grown twisted and confusing. The term *bad guy* could be used to describe Griff on days when he manipulated and lied to achieve his mission.

The mission of protecting innocents was all that mattered, Griff reminded himself. Who better to slay demons than Griff, a man with nothing to lose?

His gaze drifted to the next case, displaying a mini scene of a soda shop from the 1960s. The dolls looked so alive and cheerful. Two little girls sat at the counter, one eyeing a glass goblet filled with ice cream.

Yes, he could see why people were drawn to this fantasy world of pleasantries and hope. Creating these scenes gave one the illusion of being in control, made all the wrongs right.

He may never be able to make things right in his own life, but he could make things right for his country by finding the microchip and saving lives.

He'd start by getting more details about the redhead's life, her fears, hopes and desires, using that information to get close to her. Hell, maybe he'd even make her fall in love with him—Griffin Black, the software engineer, eligible bachelor and all-around gentleman. He enjoyed getting into character, pretending to be something he definitely was not.

"Time to get started," he whispered and headed downstairs.

"'I'LL BE downstairs working and stuff?'" Ciara repeated, adjusting the gold, shimmering gown on the Tonner doll in the gift shop. "I sounded like an idiot."

The handsome stranger with the piercing blue eyes had rattled her. First of all, few men risked venturing into a doll museum. She thought it sweet he was interested in a doll for his daughter.

She realized she was grossly out of practice communicating with the opposite sex. Truth was she hadn't had much time for conversation with men since she took over the museum.

She fingered the fairy charm at the base of her neck and eyed the doll. "Perfect."

"Kind of like our male visitor?" Adele said, walking into the room.

"Stop," Ciara warned.

Adele, bless her, was one of Gran's best friends and worked for practically nothing.

Tipping her head to the side, Ciara studied her most recent delivery. The Tonner dolls were going to be a big seller. They had to be.

"Well?" Adele asked, organizing the display of miniature hairbrushes, purses and scarves on the glass counter.

"Well, what?" Ciara said, glancing at the elderly woman.

"What did you find out about Frank Sinatra?"

"Who?"

"The man upstairs?"

"He looks nothing like Frank Sinatra." And he didn't. Sinatra had a young, mischievous look to him, whereas the man named Griffin looked...dangerous.

Girl, at this point they all seem dangerous.

They'd continue to seem dangerous unless she got some practice and threw herself into the dating pool. She wasn't looking forward to getting hurt again. Thom's betrayal still stung, even though it had been eight months ago.

"His eyes were sky blue like Frank's," Adele argued.

"True."

"So, you noticed?" Adele smiled.

Ciara planted her hands to her hips. "He's in town on business and is going to buy a doll for his daughter. He's married."

"Did he say he was married?"

"No, but, just stop. I'm not interested."

"Why on earth not? You need some recreation in your life. You've turned into a workaholic."

"No lectures. I get enough of those from mom." Even though her mother had retired to Arizona with her new boyfriend, the phone lines still burned with lectures on her not living forever and Ciara needing to produce some cute, cuddly grandchildren. It was, after all, always about Mom, not about Ciara's needs or desires. Sure she wanted children, but first she'd have to find a man she could trust enough in order to fall in love. Not likely.

"Not to change the subject, but the furnace is making those noises again," Adele warned.

"The clicking ones?"

"The coughing-gagging ones. If you don't replace that thing it's going to blow up the entire block."

"It's tops on the list."

"Have you got Amelia's party on your list? My granddaughter is so passionate about dolls. She's a sweet girl, like you."

Yep, that was Ciara: sweet, caring and determined to keep Gran's doll-shop dream alive.

"It's on my calendar," Ciara said, avoiding a direct answer. She didn't want to hurt the woman's feelings, but she had so much paperwork to catch up on, plus she had to prepare for the board meeting Monday, and still had the menu to go over for the Prendegrast party.

She wondered what Gran would think of her opening the lower level for private parties. Well, Ciara had to do something to keep Ruth's Doll Emporium in the black. When she'd taken over six months ago, it was apparent that Gran wasn't the best bookkeeper or manager, but she loved her museum and had left it to Ciara as an act of love.

Adele leaned into the counter. "Ruth wouldn't have wanted you to sacrifice your life for her dream."

"No worries. I'm not sacrificing. For your information, I have a date Sunday with Dean Monroe."

"No kidding?" Adele's eyes lit up.

Ciara didn't mention that Dean was her accountant and they were going to discuss how to keep the museum profitable for another month.

"I can see it now," Ciara said. "You're already picking out china."

"It's been so long since I've been to a wedding," Adele said.

"Well, mine isn't happening anytime soon."

The telephone rang, thank goodness. Ciara didn't like conflict, especially with a friend like Adele.

Ciara answered the phone. "Ruth's Doll Emporium."

"Ciara, it's Pete Desai. There's a problem with your server, so I'll be shutting down the Web site this afternoon for an hour to tweak some things. That work for you?"

"Sure, thanks, Pete. By the way, I'm still waiting on your bill from last month."

"Buy me lunch?"

She smiled to herself. Pete was a nice kid, although a little young for her. Besides, she wasn't ready for another romantic disaster. *Coward.*

"How about next week?" Ciara winked at Adele.

"Great. Thursday?"

"Perfect, thanks."

She hung up and smiled at Adele. "Pete and I are going to lunch next week."

"The computer geek? Isn't he a little young for you?"

"Now you're screening my prospects?" she joked.

"Of course not." Adele glanced out the glass window into the hallway and sighed. "Here comes the queen."

Ciara glanced up to greet Lucinda, an attractive middle-aged woman with too much time on her hands and enough money to support a small country. Ciara was lucky to have her as a benefactor.

"Girls, girls, girls," Lucinda said, with a dramatic wave of her manicured fingers. "Have I got news…"

"Another fiancé?" Adele offered.

Adele and Lucinda never got along, even though Lucinda had done so much for the museum.

"Good to see you, Lucinda," Ciara said. "What's the news?"

Lucinda, dressed in a sharp burgundy suit, heels and matching hat, eyed Adele and snapped her attention to

Ciara. "I've acquired two dolls, perfect for the museum. They're vintage Shirley Temple, sure to bring collectors into the shop."

"Fantastic," Ciara said. Lucinda tended to exaggerate, but Ciara appreciated her enthusiasm.

"I've had the dolls shipped to the museum. Call me when they arrive and we'll discuss the best way to display them."

One thing Ciara was good at was displaying the dolls, but she didn't want to argue with the generous woman.

"Great, thanks," Ciara said. Now the sticky part. "I hate to ask, but—"

"I've covered all fees, dear. Don't worry your pretty freckles over this acquisition. It's wonderful. Until tomorrow, then."

Lucinda started to leave and hesitated when her eyes caught the Tonner collection. She smirked over her shoulder at Adele and breezed out of the shop.

"Witch," Adele muttered.

"Why do you dislike her so much?"

"Let's see, for starters, she's rude, rich, arrogant and has no sense of self-awareness." She straightened a stack of museum brochures.

"And she's one of our most generous supporters."

"Because she wants something," Adele said, pointing a brochure at Ciara. "I heard her daughter recently got engaged. I'll bet she wants to host the reception downstairs for free."

"I'm sure she'll want something more grand," Ciara said. The lower level of the museum was charming, but not classy enough for a woman of Lucinda's means.

"She also uses men."

"Adele!"

"She does. She's been married four times. That's not normal."

"She's had bad luck with men." Ciara readjusted a lavender gown on a princess doll. "You can't blame her for that."

But Ciara blamed herself for not keeping Thom happy.

The worst of it was the lying, Thom telling her he loved her while meeting Ciara's friend Susan for coffee. Not only had Ciara lost a fiancé, but she'd lost a friend, as well.

"Back to your love life," Adele pushed.

"I'd like to keep that private, thank you."

"As long as you don't end up a lonely old lady, like me."

"I thought you liked your independence?"

"Oh, I do, but sometimes it would be nice to have a companion to boss around."

"Is that what men are for?" Ciara chuckled.

"That and to mooch off of."

"Adele," Ciara scolded.

"What? We'll never make the kind of salaries they do. I hate having to worry about paying my credit card bill every month."

"I'm sorry. I wish I could increase your salary."

"Oh, pishaw." She waved her hand. "Don't feel bad about my spending habits. Anyway, you find yourself a nice, rich man, hear?"

"There are worse things than being alone."

"Name one."

"Giving your heart to a liar," she let slip.

Adele shot her a look of pity.

"Hey, don't feel sorry for me. I think I'd make a perfect old maid." She snatched a scarf from the rack and draped it across her shoulders. "I'd be eccentric yet glamorous, don't you think?" She twirled and froze at the sight of the stranger from upstairs standing in the doorway.

Adele giggled and said, "What do you think, sir? Glamorous?"

Ciara felt completely naked.

"Not exactly," he said with a smile.

Embarrassed, she unwrapped the scarf from her neck.

"More like, charming," he offered.

She blushed again. Drat, she had to get out more, be around men so she didn't react like a thirteen-year-old.

"How can we help you?" Adele offered, because Ciara seemed to have lost her ability to speak.

"I'm looking for a gift for my daughter," he said, walking toward Ciara.

Her heart raced. There was something about this ruggedly handsome man that made her nervous.

She turned to place the scarf back on the rack.

"How old is she?" Adele asked.

He hesitated for a second and Ciara turned to look at him.

"Ten," he said, holding her gaze.

She warmed under his scrutiny.

"What about this one?" Griffin said, reaching out to touch the gown on the Tonner doll. His fingers were long and gentle as they brushed against the fabric. Ciara couldn't tear her gaze from his hand.

Adele cleared her throat, snapping Ciara out of her trance. "I guess it depends on if you're buying it for her to play with or simply admire," Adele said.

"Admire, definitely." He shot Ciara that cryptic smile again.

Was he flirting with her? Sure, why not, he was in

town on business, was probably lonely and could use a little female company.

But casual sex wasn't Ciara's thing. His blue eyes darkened as if he'd sensed the direction of her thoughts.

"This is a beautiful doll," he said, nodding at the Tonner. "But I'd like something a little less flashy, more down-to-earth." He eyed her. "A girl-next-door type, know what I mean?"

With her petite features and fair skin, she'd been put in that category more than once: the girl next door with a trusting heart.

A heart that got crushed beyond repair.

"We received a new shipment today. Let me see if there's anything that would be suitable." Ciara practically sprinted to the storeroom, but didn't miss Adele's wink or the fluttering in her own stomach. This wasn't fear, exactly. It was…excitement.

Of course she was excited. This was more male attention than she was used to, that's all.

Ciara slipped into the storage closet and shut the door. The small room filled with dolls reminded her of playing make-believe with Gran. They'd spin wonderful stories about beautiful princesses being saved by white knights. Ciara believed the fantasies could come true—until she was thirteen and her mom and dad split, leaving her torn between two warring parents.

She'd never do that to her children. Heck, she'd never marry a domineering, controlling man like Dad. She sighed. Sometimes she wondered if her expectations were simply too high.

"Back to work." She searched the boxes for a "girl-next-door" doll for the stranger named Griffin.

She found an American Girl Mia doll complete with ice skates and long, blond hair. "Perfect."

The door cracked open and Adele poked her head inside. "It's safe."

"Safe?"

"A handsome man flirts with you and you go running off into the closet?"

"I did not." Ciara walked back into the shop. "Where did he go?"

"Got a phone call and had to leave."

Ciara went to the window and glanced into the parking lot. Griffin was talking on his cell phone as he approached an expensive car.

"Do you seriously think he was flirting?" she let slip.

"Honey, I may be pushing seventy, but I know flirting when I see it. Yes, definitely."

Ciara studied the man, about six feet tall with broad shoulders, wearing a dark leather jacket. Even from this vantage point she could make out his square jaw covered with two days' growth of beard.

Adele sighed. "Eye candy."

Ciara smacked the woman in the shoulder. "Hey!"

"Don't you ever get tired of work, work, work and no playing around?" Adele said.

"Don't have time to think about it."

She glanced outside. Griffin suddenly looked up, and she stepped away from the window.

"You can't hide behind your pain forever," Adele said. "Thom was a jerk. Move on."

"I will, when I'm ready."

Adele went back behind the counter. "Mr. Blue Eyes said he might stop by later. This is your chance to climb back on the horse and get some practice."

"I don't need practice. I need a nice guy who's good with children, takes care of his mom and is honest to a fault. Someone who will make me pancakes, bring me flowers for no reason and put up with my moods."

"Honey, Prince Charming is a fantasy. Didn't anyone ever tell you that?"

"WE NEED the job done by Monday," Griff's supervisor said.

Cell phone in his hand, Griff glanced up at the gray sky. "What's happened?"

"Our source says the terrorists plan to install the microchip into a 767 jet engine, which goes onto the assembly line Monday morning. We need to retrieve the chip before we're unable to identify which plane it's in."

"Can't you track it?"

"Not after it's been installed. Too much electronic activity would interfere with the digital recorder. Have you made progress?"

Griff glanced at the museum window. "Yes, sir."

He'd made contact with the owner and charmed her, but hadn't planned on moving quite so fast. Monday was only five days away.

"I'll need a daily update," his boss added.

Griff stiffened. "Daily?"

"Yes."

What the hell? Didn't they trust him? "I understand," Griff said, yet he didn't.

The line went dead, and Griff shoved the phone into his pocket. He was methodical about his jobs, creating a foolproof plan before going in for the kill.

Hell, he hoped he didn't have to kill the cute redhead in the museum. "Not good," he whispered, realizing

Ciara had somehow roused his compassion. He was shocked he still recognized the feeling.

Griff got into the BMW and punched in the code on his laptop. He needed to find out every intimate detail about Ms. O'Malley in order to streamline their relationship and get the chip.

In minutes he had Intel about her background, schooling, siblings and boyfriends.

"Broke up with fiancé eight months ago and hasn't dated since," he murmured aloud. He knew how rebound relationships were quick, intense and painful.

It was the perfect description of what he was about to do, but he didn't feel any guilt. After all, she was selling goods to the enemy.

He mapped out a plan for the next few days, starting with his next Ciara encounter. He'd return at closing to catch her one more time, offer to purchase a doll for his fictitious daughter and charm her a bit more. He'd invite her to dinner, get her to drink a little and loosen up.

The woman was wound tighter than a baseball. Why? Had she been notified that an NSA agent had been dispatched to shut down her operation?

He still couldn't believe how American citizens betrayed their own country in such brutal ways. Manipulating a plane to crash and kill innocents: mothers, wives, sisters.

He shook off the memory of the phone call about Beth. From that day forward he'd made a commitment to honor her death by defeating the enemy. He'd joined AW-21 and pledged to do whatever was necessary to save innocents like his big sister.

In this case if it meant being ruthless with a charming redhead like Ciara to achieve his goal, then so be it.

Chapter Two

Ciara had finished most of her projects, from ordering food for the Prendegrast fund-raiser, to analyzing the budget to determining ways to cut overhead. She had to dip into the foundation reserve again to cover her costs. How had Gran kept the museum going without it?

She glanced at the box delivered an hour ago courtesy of Lucinda. Thank goodness for wealthy friends of the museum who donated their time and money to help keep the museum afloat.

The reality was, Ciara wasn't sure how much longer she could keep it going.

"Think positive," she encouraged herself.

She had some good plans in motion like promoting the party space and hosting silent auctions and educational seminars.

But dolls were a niche market, even Gran knew that, and in the end, she'd had to invest all her savings into the museum.

Ciara's gaze drifted to the photo of her and Gran from two years ago. Gran had been a calming, positive influence in Ciara's life when Ciara struggled with teenage crises on her own. She didn't blame her mom for not being there emotionally. Her mother had her own grief to work through after having been blind-sided by Ciara's controlling dad. They'd been married nearly twenty years when he'd come home and announced he was moving to San Diego with his girlfriend.

At thirteen, Ciara had been unable to make sense of the abandonment. He was her father, and he'd betrayed her in the worst way.

This was why she'd avoided serious relationships for so long. It wasn't until she'd met kind, quiet Thom that she thought loving someone for a lifetime was possible.

What a fool. She should have seen it coming, but how could she when he showered her with his endearing charm and attention?

The phone rang, shaking her from her thoughts.

"Ruth's Doll Emporium."

"You're still there?" Adele accused.

"Just about to leave."

"You should have left an hour ago."

"Yes, Mother," Ciara joked. In reality she didn't mind the older woman's concern.

"Seriously, Ciara, I worry about you. This is exactly why Ruthie wanted me to run the museum after her passing. She knew I could keep my private life separate from the museum, whereas you've buried yourself in the business."

Adele was right. The museum had become Ciara's life. Pathetic.

"I'll be leaving shortly, promise."

"Speaking of promises, did Lucinda's dolls arrive, or was she playing with us?"

"I got the box this afternoon. Haven't had a chance to open it."

"And you won't because you're hanging up and heading straight home."

Right, to an empty apartment. She could hardly wait.

Adele must have sensed Ciara's thoughts. "Or you could stop by my place for dinner. I made Chicken Catch a Louie."

Ciara smiled. Adele was always the adventurous cook. "No, thanks. I've got—" she hesitated, almost saying she had work to do, but realized she'd get another lecture if she let that slip. "I'm looking forward to a quiet evening in front of the TV."

"All right, see you tomorrow. I'm on the schedule to open if you want to sleep in."

"Thanks, Adele, for everything."

"My pleasure. And if you change your mind and want me to take over for a few weeks, say the word."

"Thanks, you're the best."

Ciara hung up and her gaze caught on the box containing Lucinda's new acquisitions. She was dying to peek inside, but if she was ever going to close up, she'd better take the box home and open it there.

First, she'd have to make her last round and polish the display cases so they'd be set for Adele to open tomorrow. She went upstairs and started on the glass. Who was she kidding? A dozen people had walked through her doors today and only half had gone upstairs to the museum. The rest went directly to the gift shop to buy dolls.

Which reminded her of Mr. Blue Eyes, as Adele named him. He'd said he might stop by later, but never showed. Ciara glanced at the clock more than once wondering if he'd walk through her front door again.

Silly girl. Now she was fantasizing about a perfect stranger.

A muted beep echoed from down the hall. "What the heck?"

She started toward it, wondering if someone left a cell phone behind or if the security system's battery was low. It's not like Gran had installed a high-tech system because the building was located in a busy section of Bellevue. Another reason why Ciara kept getting offers to buy the place. The museum sat on prime real estate.

But it had been Gran's dream that the museum stay where it was, in an old house, an original in the neighborhood. Even when others were torn down to make room for strip malls and condos, Gran held firm and had the cottage plaqued to help preserve its integrity.

The high-pitched tone sounded again and Ciara followed it into the 1950s-vintage-doll room. In the corner on the floor lay a small beeper.

She picked it up. One of her visitors must have dropped it. "Huh." She shoved it into her sweater pocket and started down the stairs.

A clicking sound made her freeze. She'd locked the front door, hadn't she? Yes, yes, she was sure she had. She slowly went downstairs, slipping her cell phone from her pocket. Adrenaline rushed through her blood as she pressed 9-1-1. With her finger on the Send button, she stepped onto the first floor tile and held her breath.

Waited.

Took another deep breath.

Finger on the green button.

Ready to call police.

The rhythmic clicking echoed down the hall. She followed the sound, seeing shadows behind every corner. *Grow up, it's a doll museum. Who would want to break in?*

She peeked around the corner into the break room and smelled burning coffee. She closed her phone. "Adele," she whispered. The woman must have forgotten to turn off the coffee maker again. Ciara wasn't sure how much longer Mr. Coffee would survive.

She rinsed out the pot, and it steamed in protest. The machine continued to click, so she unplugged it, left the pot soaking and headed back to her office.

She needed to get out of here, relax and get some dinner.

She needed to get a life. On long days like this she was tempted to sell the museum. But she couldn't betray Gran's dream like that.

Locking her office, she glanced through the glass door at the box of Lucinda's dolls on her desk. She unlocked the door, grabbed the box and headed out. Curiosity was killing her about the new acquisitions, what they looked like and how much publicity they'd bring to the museum.

With the package tucked under her arm, she locked the front door and set the alarm.

She headed for her car, thinking about how they'd promote the dolls to bring in new customers. They'd developed quite a reputation for being one of the finest museums in the country. She was proud that doll enthusiasts from all over the world marked Ruth's Doll Emporium on their lists of "Must Sees."

She unlocked her car and sensed something behind her. Suddenly she was shoved up against the window.

"Hey, what the—"

Pinned to her car from behind, a male voice said, "I'm here for the product. That it in your hand?"

"What do you want with—"

He wrapped his arm around her neck and she struggled for air. This couldn't be happening, right? Who would attack her for a few dolls? She'd report it and the thief wouldn't be able to sell them without being caught and—

Unless he knew she wouldn't be alive to report it.

"No," she grunted, but it came out as a gasp. Streetlights blurred and the sound of a honking car grew louder.

This is it. I'm going to die protecting Shirley Temple dolls.

"Hey!" another male voice called.

Suddenly she was shoved head first into the doorframe and snapped back. She lost her balance and collapsed on the ground.

This had to be a bad dream. Sure, she'd gone home, had frozen enchiladas for dinner and watched *Dancing with the Stars*. She must have drifted off and something in the enchiladas hadn't agreed with her.

"You okay?"

She blinked and focused on the amazing color of Griffin's blue eyes. At least the dream was improving.

"Ciara?" he said with a frown.

She swallowed back her shock. "Is this…a dream?"

"No, unfortunately not." He reached out and stroked her hairline. "You're going to have a nasty bruise."

She touched her forehead and winced.

"Can you stand?"

She sat up and he helped her to her feet. Wobbling, she took a breath and collapsed.

GRIFF STOOD beside her in the emergency room, holding her hand. What else could he to do? She'd passed out in his arms. He couldn't leave her unconscious in the parking lot, so he'd called 9-1-1.

While he'd waited for the ambulance to come he'd had the perfect chance to snatch her package and take off. But he couldn't be sure the microchip was inside, even though he suspected as much. Why else was she brutalized for it?

When she'd spotted him at the hospital she'd reached for him, her savior. Fine, he'd play along. Especially because it would help him find the microchip quicker if she thought him an honorable gentleman instead of her enemy.

"You have a slight concussion, but more likely you fainted due to fright," the doctor said.

"Doctor Arndt," a nurse said coming around the curtain. "The police are here."

A tall, skinny cop with a long face and receding hairline stepped into the examining area.

Griff stood to leave, to give them privacy, but she held on to his hand. "Stay?"

He nodded and sat beside her.

"Ms. O'Malley, I'm Officer Banks. Could you tell me what happened?"

"I don't remember, exactly," she said.

Interesting, Griff thought.

"Tell me what you *do* remember," the officer pushed.

"I locked up the museum and went to my car. Someone came up behind me and—" She paused. "—I don't know what happened. Then I was looking up, into *his* eyes." She smiled at Griff.

The officer focused his attention on Griff. "Sir?"

"A man shoved her against the car pretty hard. I got out of my car and went to help."

"Can you describe the attacker?"

Ciara shuddered at the mention of the word *attacker.*

"About five-ten, husky build, wearing a stocking cap and camouflage jacket," Griff said.

"Good description." The cop eyed Griff.

"I play a lot of I Spy with my daughter."

"Did you hear him say anything?" the cop asked.

"No, I wasn't close enough."

"And you were at the museum after closing because...?"

"I'd been there earlier and was called away on business before I could purchase a doll for my daughter. I came back and noticed the museum was closed. That's when I spotted Miss O'Malley in the parking lot."

The officer nodded. "In case I need to contact you?"

Griff pulled a business card from his pocket. Not easy with one hand. Ciara wasn't letting go of his other one. He handed the card, complete with fake title, company name and phone number, to the officer.

The cop turned back to Ciara. "You still have your purse?"

She glanced at it. "Yes."

"Did he say anything? Anything to indicate if this was a random attack or if he wanted something specific?"

"No, I...can't remember. I think he did say something. I..." She blinked and pressed her head to the pillow. "I wish I could remember."

The cop gave her his card. "If you think of anything else."

"Thanks."

The cop nodded and left. Good. Seemed simple enough.

"Well, Miss O'Malley, everything checks out," the doctor said. "The head injury isn't serious."

"It feels serious. I have a serious headache."

"That's to be expected," the doctor assured. "You may want to check with your internist in a day or two. I'll forward the information to her."

"Great, thanks." She slipped her hand from Griff's and swung her legs over the side of the table.

"You're not going to collapse on me again, are you?" he joked.

"I don't plan on it."

He handed her the package and her purse. "Who should I call?"

"For what?" She pushed aside the curtain and headed for the hospital lobby.

"To take care of you."

"I can take care of myself, thanks."

"What about the grandmother-type in the gift shop?"

She hesitated and glanced at him. She looked so distressed that she almost had him believing she was an innocent victim. She had to know sooner or later her sins would catch up with her.

"I can't call Adele. She'd completely freak out."

"A friend?" he offered, leading her to the exit.

"Nope."

"What, you don't have any?"

She smiled at that one. "I'll be fine. Where's the payphone? I need to call a taxi."

"You're kidding, right?"

She narrowed her eyes at him. "What?"

"You fainted in my arms, I held your hand in the E.R. The least I can do is give you a ride home."

"No, I couldn't ask that of you."

He wondered if someone was waiting at her place to take the package off her hands.

"Why not?" he pushed.

She sighed and glanced at him. "I feel bad enough that I've dragged you into this."

"You make it sound like it's your fault you were assaulted. I wouldn't be a proper gentleman if I didn't see this through to the end. What would my Aunt Miriam think?"

He got another smile from that comment.

"Okay, if you're sure it's not an imposition."

"Not at all. I can take that to the car, if you'd like." He motioned to the box.

"I can make it."

"I'd rather you wait here. The garage is a bit of a hike."

She nodded and handed him the box. Just like that.

Interesting. She trusted him with the contraband. Sure, why not? He was her rescuer. She had no clue he was an enemy agent.

He went to the garage and hesitated before picking her up. He could open the box and dig into the contents, he thought.

Yet she'd given the box to him without much of a protest, which meant it had to be a decoy. He couldn't risk blowing his cover at this point.

He pulled around the circle drive and got out to open the door for her.

"Thanks," she said. "I'm four blocks north of the museum, off Bellevue Way."

Ciara didn't speak for the next few minutes. He'd ask her a question and she'd respond with a nod, as if deep in thought. Was she trying to figure out how to dump him before he dropped her off at home?

No, he had to get into her apartment and earn her trust even more. Present himself as a gallant gentleman.

"Turn right at the next driveway," she said. "I'm in building B."

He found a spot in front of her building and turned to her. "I'm going to walk you to your apartment, no arguments."

She nodded.

He helped her out of the car and carried the box as she led him to her second-floor apartment. Her fingers trembled as she stuck the key into the lock.

"Need help?"

"I can do it!" She closed her eyes and sighed. "I'm sorry. I'm just…I'm sorry."

"No problem. You've been through a traumatic experience."

When she opened the door, he was shocked that she motioned for him to come inside.

"I don't know about you, but I could use a cup of tea," she said, dropping her purse on the kitchen counter.

Tea? A bit weak for Griff.

"Sounds good," he said. "I'll make it. You sit down." He placed the package on the counter next to her purse.

"If you do that I'll really feel guilty," she said.

"You can make it up to me." He shot her a mischievous smile. "Give me a discount on one of those Tonner dolls for my daughter."

"What kind of discount?" She eyed him.

"Fifteen percent?"

"I can do that." She collapsed into a violet, thick-cushioned chair he suspected was her favorite.

He filled the teakettle and turned on the burner, then went in search of teabags.

"Drawer next to the sink," she said, tipping her head back against the thick cushions.

He found her assortment of teas. "Any preference?"

"Green."

Her cell phone rang. She got up and took it from her coat pocket. "Hello? Oh for Pete's sake, how did you find out? She's such a gossip. I'm fine, really. Yes, luckily Mr. Blue— I mean Mr. Black came back for a doll and saved me from the mugger." She glanced at Griff and smiled, that charming, beguiling smile. For a second he wished it were genuine.

"What?" she said, turning away from him and heading down the hall.

He guessed it was the grandmotherly type from the museum.

A moment later he heard the water go on in the bathroom. He eyed the package. It would take a second to cut it open and analyze its contents. If dolls were inside, he could run the digital reader across the eyes to determine if the microchip was hidden there. Although the device could read through glass, he'd bet they'd packaged the dolls in a special material that could prevent the reader from registering an affirmative signal.

If he ripped into the package and it was the wrong doll, he'd be screwed. *Patience.*

Not one of his strengths, patience was even harder to find with innocent lives on the line.

Ciara came back into the living room pointing a can of hairspray at Griff. "What do you want?"

"Excuse me?"

"You're a lying, manipulating…" Her breath caught. "Who the hell knows what you are? That was Adele on the phone. She said Miriam Anderson doesn't have a nephew named Griffin."

Damn, had his people screwed up his background? No, they were impeccable. At this point it didn't matter. Ciara saw him as the enemy. So much for seducing her.

"Go!" she shouted, pointing the hairspray at him with a trembling hand.

"I'm sorry, but I can't do that."

Chapter Three

"Why not?" Ciara asked, her voice shaking.

"Because I won't leave you alone in this condition."

Good save.

"Your friend doesn't remember me because we moved away from my Aunt Miriam's family when I was young. My mother and Miriam had a falling out and didn't talk much after that. Call Aunt Miriam, if you want. She'll confirm I am who I say I am."

It was a bluff, but he had to try. He reached for his PDA.

"What are you doing?" she said, fear in her voice.

"My phone. I've got her number in my contacts list. What, you think I'm going to pull a gun or something?"

He'd left the weapon in the car, figuring he didn't want her seeing it and growing suspicious.

Frozen in place, she aimed the hairspray at him.

"Or I can prove it to you," he said.

"How?"

"I know things about your grandmother that only her best friend would know."

"Like what?"

"Your grandmother called Miriam 'Mimi.' She was the only person who called her that."

She didn't move. "What else do you know?"

"I reunited with Miriam last year, wanting to reestablish some family ties. She told me how proud your grandmother was of your work as a preschool teacher, but she was worried about you, too."

"Worried?"

"Something about a fiancé breaking up with you?"

"Everyone knows about that."

"What possible motive would I have to take you to the hospital, bring you home, make you tea? I'm not here to harm you, Ciara. But if you want me to go, I will."

Ciara's shoulders sagged. "I'm sorry. I'm just—"

"Upset. Understandable. Sit down. I'll pour the tea."

And add a little sedative, he thought. He wouldn't seduce her while under the influence, but he could persuade her to open the box so he could determine if it contained the microchip.

Guilt snagged his conscience. Maybe it wasn't the best idea to drug her after the knock to the head. Yet he had to convince her to open the box. If he could see the dolls, run the D.R. across the eyes, he could find the chip and get the hell out of here, get away from the seemingly fragile Ciara.

He wondered how she was going to figure out which doll the chip was in or if she already knew. The smugglers had been clever about communication, not speaking in direct terms over phone or through e-mail. The red flag popped up last week when an e-mail sent from info@Ruthsdolls.com read: *Glad to help with the chip project.* Followed by a reply from the terrorist e-mail that read: *Expect by next Friday.*

Friday. The day after tomorrow.

He poured tea and brought her a mug.

She glanced up at him with such gratitude in her eyes. "Thanks. Sorry about before."

"Don't worry about it. I'd be suspicious of everything if I'd been mugged."

She nodded and sipped her tea.

"So, what's in the box?" he said.

"Dolls, what else?"

"You always bring work home with you?"

"Don't start."

Mug in hand, he sat opposite the coffee table from her. "Don't start what?"

"Giving me a hard time about working too much. I get daily lectures from Adele."

"She worries about you?"

"Like a fretting mother." She fingered the rim of her cup. "I guess it's okay, because my mom isn't here anymore."

"Passed away?"

"Moved to Arizona."

He nodded and sipped his tea. Ciara looked like she could use a mother right about now. Someone to take care of her other than Griff, who had his own agenda.

It's all lies. Don't get sucked in.

He stood and went to the kitchen. "Want something to eat?"

He opened the fridge and was greeted by an expired carton of eggs, expired milk and various half-empty bottles of condiments.

"There's cereal in the cabinet." She sighed. "What I wouldn't give for something hot."

"I could get takeout," he offered.

"I couldn't impose like that."

"Sure you could. I'm hungry, too."

"Only if you'll let me pay."

"But—"

"I insist." She sat straight.

"Okay. Wouldn't want you to come at me with the hairspray again," he joked.

"Ah, I'm so embarrassed."

"Don't be. I noticed a Thai place a few blocks from here."

"Sounds great. Pad thai is my favorite."

"You sure you'll be okay by yourself?"

"Positive, thanks."

"Back in ten. Lock the door behind me."

She got up and followed him to the door. "Thanks," she said.

With a nod, he headed for the car. Instinct told him not to leave, that in the few minutes it would take for him to get the food she could hand off the dolls. He called in the order and asked that it be delivered, planning to pay the driver, and make it seem like he'd gone out to pick it up.

A text message beeped. His supervisor needed him to call in.

"Black."

"We've intercepted another e-mail."

"And?"

"They've sent three microchips, not one."

Three chips. Three planes. Hell.

"If you need backup, Agent Keen is in the area. I'll text you his number."

"Yes, sir."

Moving his car to the far corner of the lot, Griff burned at the latest news: three microchips would be used to kill innocents. And he had seventy-two hours to track them down.

A few minutes later a brown Ford Taurus pulled into the lot and parked outside Ciara's building. Thinking it was the delivery driver, he started to get out of his car, then noticed the supposedly traumatized Ciara push through the front door of her apartment looking energized and perky.

She'd been playing him, all right. And to think a part of him wished she was an innocent woman struggling to save her grandmother's business. He noticed she didn't carry the box of dolls. Must have been a decoy. She got into the car and it drove off.

He followed the car to the museum and parked a safe distance away. He watched Ciara go inside, but still couldn't get a good look at her accomplice. Then he noticed the squad car parked on the street. Bellevue PD must be keeping an eye on things after tonight's assault on Ciara.

Five minutes later Ciara came out carrying a package under her arm. Bingo. Must be the chips. She said something to the driver, but got into her own car with the package. What the hell?

Griff followed her back to the apartment complex and watched Ciara go inside. He'd bet his pension the small package had the microchipped dolls inside.

He pulled his Glock from the glove box and tucked it into his belt. No reason to play the helpful stranger anymore. He stood beneath the overhang of her building waiting for the Thai delivery, figuring it was the simplest way back into her apartment.

Once inside he'd lay it out for her: the microchip in exchange for her life. Then it was up to the U.S. Government how it wanted to punish her for treason.

The terrorists had done a fine job of finding the perfect, innocent-looking female to smuggle goods into the country. No one would suspect Miss Ciara O'Malley, former preschool teacher, of espionage.

The delivery driver pulled up. Griff paid him and headed upstairs. He'd love nothing more than a quick end to this assignment. He couldn't stand being drawn in by Ciara's enchanting green eyes and sweet voice. What he wouldn't give for the truth for a change, a real life.

A real life? Where had that come from?

He knocked. "Ciara? Food's here."

Nothing.

"Ciara?" he said again.

He placed his hand on his gun. She couldn't suspect he was an agent, unless he'd been compromised.

"Ciara!" he said with more force.

The door swung open and a husky guy with a scar running across his cheek glared at Griff. The guy looked like the mugger from last night.

"She's not here." Husky guy eyed the carryout bag. "Thanks." He snatched the bag and started to shut the door. Griff shouldered it open and marched into her apartment.

"Where is she?"

"Gone. She asked me to watch the place."

"I doubt that."

"Get lost." He shoved Griff at the door, but Griff caught the guy's wrist and twisted, bringing him to his knees.

"Who are you?"

"Screw you."

"No, thanks." Griff knocked him out with the butt of his pistol.

Glock in hand, he made his way down the hall to the bedroom. He toed open the door with his boot, but it was empty. He noticed the bathroom door was closed. Had the guy already killed her and was in the process of dismembering her body? Why, because she thought she could raise the price?

He opened the door and found her gagged and flexicuffed to the exposed sink pipes. Her eyes widened in fear at the sight of his gun. Slipping it back into the holster, he kneeled beside her and slid the gag from her mouth.

"He was…he hit me…"

Griff sat back against the pale pink wall and crossed his arms against his chest. "What did you think he was going to do? What did you do, find a higher bidder and thought you could betray them?"

"What are you talking about?"

"No more games. I'm an NSA agent. Where are the chips?"

"You're a…?"

"Freelancer for the NSA. I'm assuming your friend in the living room was sent to pick up the goods."

She shook her head. "What goods?"

"I said, no more games!" he shouted.

She cringed and closed her eyes. "Don't hurt me."

"That's up to you. Give me the microchips and I'm gone."

"I don't know what you're talking about," she said with pleading green eyes.

"Yeah?" He leaned close. "Who picked you up in the Ford just now?"

"Adele. The alarm went off at the museum. She couldn't reactivate it, so she called me."

"You looked awfully happy when you got into her car."

"I didn't want her to be overly concerned about what happened to me earlier," she explained.

"You walked out of the museum with a package."

"You followed me?"

"It's my job. I'm not your friend, Ciara. I'm not Aunt Miriam's nephew. I'm a government agent. Now tell me where the chip is."

"I swear on Gran's grave, I don't know what you're talking about."

He chuckled. "Now that's rich. One traitor swearing on another traitor's grave."

"I'm not a traitor. Neither was she! You've got the wrong family."

"Yeah? Where's the package you brought home from the museum just now?"

"On my dresser. It's a doll Adele asked me to spruce up for her granddaughter's birthday."

When he stood, she cowered, as if she thought he was going to hit her. He went to her bedroom and found the package where she said it would be. Bringing it into the bathroom, he wondered if the goon in the living room had backup and how many.

Griff pulled out his knife and cut open the box. Foam peanuts spilled out as he dug inside and found a porcelain doll. He pulled out the card reader and scanned the doll's face. It registered a signal.

He smashed it against the tile floor.

"No!" she cried.

The doll's head split in half. A tear trailed down Ciara's cheek.

He ripped his gaze from hers and eyed the porcelain remains of the head. He fingered a small gray pouch. "What's this?" He poured the contents of the pouch into his palm. Diamonds, probably with a GPS tracking chip in one of them, which set off the card reader.

"You're a full-service smuggler, aren't you?" he said.

"No, that's not right. That's not the doll we ordered."

Her eyes teared and her lower lip quivered. God, she was good.

He was about to start his interrogation when he heard a man's voice echo from the living room.

"Not a sound." He shut the door and went to investigate. The voice was coming from a radio on the goon's belt.

"Tiger Four, come in, over.... Respond immediately or we're sending a cleanup team."

Hell. Griff went into the bathroom and pulled out his knife. Ciara closed her eyes as if she thought he was going to slit her throat.

He cut her loose. "Grab your things."

"I'm not going anywhere with you." She struggled against him.

"I'd choose me over the four guys about to storm your place. I'll be a lot nicer."

"Why is this happening?" she whimpered.

He dragged her behind him, ignoring the pain in her voice. "Get your purse and the box on the counter."

"Let me go!" She pulled away from him.

He stopped short and got in her face. "You keep resisting me and I swear I'll leave you tied up so they can find and torture you."

He motioned toward the box. She grabbed it and her purse. They stepped over the unconscious guy's body and raced to the side exit.

They made their way down the stairs and out into the cool, damp night. He hesitated before turning the corner of the apartment building, wanting to see if the enemy had identified his car. They shouldn't have, but they seemed to have excellent Intel. The parking lot was quiet.

"Come on!" he ordered, pulling her behind him to the car. He shoved her in the passenger side and got behind the wheel. They pulled out of the lot and in his rearview mirror he spied two men race out of the building. That was fast.

"Let's make this simple. Where's the microchip?" he asked.

"I don't know what you're talking about."

"We know everything, Miss O'Malley. We know you're a traitor."

"No! You've got the wrong person."

"Damn it, woman, that wasn't stuffing in that doll's head. Those were diamonds. Frankly, I don't care about diamonds or drugs or whatever else you're into, but the microchips will cost innocent people their lives. You need to tell me where they are."

"Go to hell."

HELPLESS. Confused. Devastated.

Ciara's life had been ripped apart by the handsome stranger who'd seemed so nice, so caring only hours ago.

She struggled against the duct tape he'd used to bind her to the dining room chair in his apartment. How had she gone from doll-museum owner to victim?

It had to be a case of mistaken identity.

Griffin leaned against the wall and took a swig of bourbon. She had to get through to him, convince him she was innocent. One look into his steely blue eyes and she knew that wasn't going to happen. He glared at her like she was a pedophile.

Suddenly he pushed away from the wall, placed his drink on the coffee table and closed in.

Her chest tightened. He was going to kill her.

In three steps he towered over her.

"Please don't hurt me," she squeaked.

"Tell me where to find the microchips and I won't have to hurt you."

"How would I know that?"

He crouched in front of her and squeezed her arm. "Because you took over the family business from that sweet grandmother of yours."

"Dolls, we own a doll museum."

"You're smugglers for the highest bidder."

"What are you talking about?"

"It's been going on for years. What a great cover. Granny displaying the antique dolls, selling a few on the side. All the while using blood money to pay the bills."

"Bastard!" She pulled on her bindings, wanting to smack the guy.

There was no way Gran was guilty of what he was accusing her of. She couldn't be a criminal. Gran had been the one thing in Ciara's life that had made sense when everything else had fallen apart.

"If you won't share the truth willingly, then I'll take other measures."

He stood and went into the kitchenette. She heard him unzip something, then turn on the faucet. What was he going to do to her? Her body involuntarily trembled.

He stepped into her line of vision holding a hypodermic needle.

"What's that?"

"Something to stimulate your cooperation."

"I'd cooperate if I could. I don't know anything."

He crouched beside her. "We'll see about that. Stop shaking."

"I...I can't. Don't, please don't—ouch!" He pressed the needle into her skin.

"While we wait for this to take effect, let's see what's in the box." He got the box Lucinda had sent to the shop and pulled out a knife.

"Don't break them. They're collectibles."

He hesitated and looked at her. "Where did they train you? You're so damned convincing."

"Maybe because I'm telling the truth."

"We'll find that out in a minute, won't we?"

He cut open the box and pulled out an antique Russian doll dressed in a wedding gown. This wasn't what Lucinda said she'd bought. He pulled out a second doll, a man, dressed in a tuxedo. Ciara's mind drifted to her almost-wedding. She'd planned everything from the food to the flowers and invites. They were going to have it at the museum. It would have been so beautiful.

The dolls blurred. Oh, God. She was falling under the influence of whatever drug he'd given her.

He ran his magnifying card over the doll's face. "Don't hurt him, don't hurt him," she whispered.

She closed her eyes. Couldn't watch him destroy another treasure. Men always destroyed. Your life, your heart. Dad had destroyed her family with his infidelity; Thom had destroyed her heart with his betrayal.

To think she'd been attracted to Griffin, the gentleman who'd morphed into a monster before her eyes.

"What did your grandmother tell you before she died?" Griffin said.

"Good girl, she said I was a good girl. Dad never did. Mom, where is Mom?" She squinted and glanced around the room.

"Where is the microchip?"

She laughed.

"What's so funny?"

"It's not micro. I told Mom that's all Thom could afford." She stared into the man's clear blue eyes. "Love isn't micro. It's everything. The diamond chip was everything to me."

She sighed and tipped her head back. Dizzies filled her head, but something snapped her back to earth.

"The microchips." Griff glared.

Angry eyes. Like Dad's.

"Which doll are they in?" he demanded.

"They don't put computers in dolls, except maybe the ones that eat and poop. We don't carry those. They aren't classy dolls." She sighed. "I always wanted to be classy, like Evening Gown Barbie. Long, dark hair, burgundy gown, pearls…"

"Focus!" With a firm grip of her chin, he turned her to face him.

"Okay," she said. "I'm sorry, you wanted a doll for your daughter?"

"I want the microchip."

"It's gone." She drifted.

"Gone where?"

"I sold it."

"To whom?"

Her lower lip quivered as she remembered the day she'd pawned the engagement ring Thom had given her.

"Craigslist," she confessed. "I got a hundred bucks from a high-school senior. True love. That's what he wanted it for. His true love."

She blinked, remembering what it felt like to be in love. At least she'd thought she was in love. Sadness filled her chest at the memory of seeing Thom with her friend, laughing and smiling. Then Ciara remembered his confession that tore her apart: *I guess I don't love you.*

Her relationship with Thom wasn't true love, her parents hadn't experienced true love, even Gran had married for security, not true love.

"It's a fantasy, isn't it?" she asked the man with the penetrating blue eyes. "There's no such thing as true love, is there?"

"No."

Chapter Four

He couldn't believe it. The woman was more concerned about missing out on love than giving up the information to save her life.

Unless, she had no information to give.

No, she put on a good act, but she was no innocent. Agents were trained to compartmentalize their minds, lock away the important stuff during interrogations. Even on the sodium pentothal Ciara had been able to lock away the information he needed to find the microchip.

He sipped his drink and studied the unconscious woman, wondering how she'd been drawn into this line of work. She didn't seem the type, not physically strong enough, especially because she'd been so easily subdued by the husky guy back at her apartment. That made Griff wonder. Why didn't she hand over the chips?

Because she didn't have them yet?

But when she did, Griff would be at her side ready to take them off her hands, cuff those fragile wrists and send her to jail.

She sighed and shifted uncomfortably in the chair. Hell, she wasn't going to talk in this state. He slipped his glass to the table and unbound her wrists.

"Come on." He pulled her to her feet, but her legs gave way.

When he picked her up she automatically wrapped her arms around his neck, burying her face in his shoulder. Her hair smelled of sweet flowers and an earthy spice. As he carried her to the leather couch, she nuzzled his shoulder, whispering endearments against his cotton shirt.

"Thom, make love to me."

Then she kissed his neck.

He laid her on the couch, but she wouldn't release him. Her breath warmed his skin as she whispered, "Kiss me, Thom."

Temptation clawed at his insides when he realized it had been months since he'd lost himself in mindless sex. But sex with this female couldn't be classified as mindless. He'd be consciously crossing the line, taking advantage of a woman under the influence.

Taking advantage of an enemy who wanted Griff to kiss her.

No, she didn't want Griff. She wanted her loser ex-fiancé who she obviously still loved. So sure, why not? Agents were human, vulnerable to ridiculous emotions like love.

Ciara released him and passed out, her hand knocking the coffee table as her arm went limp.

"Ciara," he said with a slight tap to her cheek.

She didn't move, didn't make a sound. He went to the kitchen and got a cold cup of water. What if the combination of the knock to her head and the powerful barbiturate really put her out? He needed her conscious to help him find the microchip.

Sitting beside her on the couch, he splashed water in her face. She moaned, but didn't open her eyes.

"Wake up." He tapped her cheek.

Nothing.

He ripped his PDA from his pocket and called in.

"Identify," the computerized voice said.

"Agent Black, number 5544."

"Extension?"

"2067."

"Lab, Kyle speaking."

"It's Agent Black. I need advice about possible side effects of sodium pentathol."

"Hang on."

Griff glanced at Ciara. Her normally rosy cheeks were pale.

"Medical history of patient?" the lab rat said.

"I don't have it."

"Then you shouldn't have administered the drug."

"I'm dealing with a Class Five terrorist alert. Save the lecture, and tell me what to do. Female, twentysomething, slim build."

"Symptoms?"

"Unconscious."

"Any other drugs in her system?"

"I don't think so."

"You need to know. Check her file and call me back."

Click.

"Worthless." Griff grabbed his laptop, sat across the coffee table from her and went to work, digging into her medical records. At fourteen she was hit by a car while running down the middle of the street. She suffered a broken leg and head injury. No indication of future complications. Maybe she was on antidepressants. It seemed to be a popular form of coping with life.

Griff emptied out her purse on the table. No pills.

Maybe she kept them at home, didn't want anyone to know she relied on drugs to get through the day. He searched her bank records, medical records, but found nothing indicating she was on medication.

He called the lab back.

"I can't find anything."

"SP isn't dangerous. You probably gave her too much. Let her sleep it off."

"I need her awake."

"You should have thought of that before you injected her."

"How long will she sleep?"

"Depending on her weight, six to ten hours."

Griff hung up, frustrated with the jerk on the other end of the line, but even more frustrated with himself. Patience had never been one of his strengths. If he hadn't been in such a damn hurry, he could have used another technique to get her help. That had been the plan originally: seduce her, earn her trust.

Instead he skipped that move and went for the jugular because it was obvious she was involved in the smuggling. She wasn't an innocent.

Or was it something else that made him avoid the seduction route? Like his unwanted attraction to this woman?

Man, she was good if she could penetrate Griff's protective shell.

With nothing to do but wait it out, he decided to get some sleep. He couldn't risk her waking up and taking off on him. He lifted her in his arms again, this time ignoring her seductive scent, and carried her to the bedroom. As he placed her on the bed, his cell vibrated with a text message.

Secondary delivery location suspected—not museum.

"Hell," he muttered. How was he going to find the delivery drop if it wasn't the museum?

Griff eyed the woman who lay unconscious on his bed. This woman was his best lead. He would keep her close.

He grabbed cuffs from his nightstand. He cuffed her wrist, slipped the other cuff through the bedpost, and cuffed his own wrist, pocketing the key. Tomorrow he'd continue his interrogation, get details about the smuggling and how she'd move the chips. He hoped she'd give up the innocent act and cooperate, make it easy on herself. In the meantime he'd get a few hours of sleep to recharge.

Hell, who was he kidding? It's not like he was going to get any sleep with her warming his bed.

That's when he admitted that deep down he wished a sweet young woman like Ciara really existed and she wasn't an illusion created by espionage. If he was thinking like that, he needed a vacation, a few months off to regain his focus. Or was he burned out? Was it time to move on to another job?

"Can't think about that now," he muttered, adjusting his body, hoping to put space between them.

Instead she stretched her free arm across his chest and sighed. It was going to be a long night.

Daddy, come back!

She raced down the street after the brown sedan, desperate to catch her dad and find out when he was coming home again. The science fair was next week at school, and the father-daughter dance and—

WHACK!

"No!" she gasped, struggling to breathe, fighting to free herself from being pinned. "I can't get up. I'm stuck, I'm—"

"Ciara!" a man shouted.

She opened her eyes. The blue-eyed bastard was pressing his body against hers, their lips an inch apart.

"What are you doing?" she said.

"Restraining you."

She glanced up at her wrist, which was cuffed to the bedpost.

"Let me go. Get off me!" She automatically jerked her knee to nail him in the crotch, but he pressed his thigh harder against her.

"You need to get off," she cried.

"Not until you calm down."

"How am I supposed calm down when you want to kill me?"

"I won't kill you as long as you help me find the microchips."

Pleading ignorance wasn't going to help her. Nothing she said would convince this jerk she wasn't a smuggler.

"I'm calm, I'm calm." She breathed between clenched teeth. "And I need to use the bathroom."

He edged off her and unlocked her cuffs. Sitting up, she rubbed her wrist where the metal had cut into her skin.

She needed to be alone, to think, figure a way out of this. Her cell phone, where was it? She'd call 9-1-1. Surely the police would rescue her.

She marched past him and he grabbed her wrist. "I don't want to hurt you," he said.

"Right." Wrenching it free, she got her purse from the living room and went into the bathroom.

She slammed the door, closed her eyes and fought

back waves of panic. She was being held captive by a violent psycho much stronger than she, with drugs and weapons and who knows what else. Eyeing herself in the mirror, she struggled to puzzle through what was happening. Why did he think she was a smuggler?

Then she remembered the diamonds. Was Gran smuggling goods into the country?

No, I can't believe it.

Diamonds? Drugs? And what was the chip Griffin kept referring to?

He banged on the door. "What are you doing in there?"

"Knitting a scarf," she shot back. Although a part of her was terrified of the man, she was furious, as well. He was responsible for turning her life upside down, accusing her and Gran of being criminals.

"Make it quick," he ordered.

She turned on the water and dug into her purse. Bingo. She found the pink cell phone. She turned it on and searched for the police officer's card from last night. Heck she didn't even know where she was, how would he save her? But you could trace cell phones, right? Sure they could. Officer Banks would rescue her from this bastard.

She made the call.

"Banks."

"It's Ciara O'Malley. I was mugged last night and you interviewed me in the hospital? You have to help me. I'm being held against my will by the man who supposedly saved me last night."

"Where?"

"I don't know."

"Stay on the line and we'll find you."

"I think he's going to kill me."

"Not if we can help it."

"Open this door, now!" Griff yelled.

She slipped the phone into her purse and whipped open the door. "Can't I wash my face?"

Griff eyed the vanity. "Leave the door open."

"Whatever." She turned to the sink and splashed water on her face. Something wasn't right. If Griff had meant to kill her, wouldn't he have done so by now?

No, he wanted something from her, something she couldn't give.

She heard a knock at the front door. Thank the heavens. She was going to be saved.

Griff hovered in the bathroom doorway. "Stay here, don't make a sound."

He shut the door.

A minute later a muffled crash echoed through the door. She cracked open the door and spotted the husky guy holding Griff while a second man slugged Griff in the stomach. What the heck? Where were the cops?

"Where's the girl?" the tall guy demanded.

"What girl?"

Griff kicked the guy in the shin and he swung in anger, giving her a clear look at his face. Ciara swallowed a gasp at the sight of Officer Banks. She'd just called him, asked him to save her...

...And he was working with the husky guy who tied her to her bathroom pipes and threatened to slice her skin?

She closed the door and pressed her forehead against the wood. Had to get out of here. Find someone to help her. Who could she trust? Not the police *or* Griff, who'd drugged and handcuffed her to his bed.

She needed to get away from them. All of them. With a deep breath, she cracked the door.

"Tell me where she is and I'll kill you quick," Officer Banks said. "Keep messing with me and I'll start by cracking your ribs, one at a time. A guy like you has to know how painful that is."

"My team took her into custody last night," Griff lied.

He was protecting her? Sure, because he thought she was a spy with information he needed to find the chip he kept talking about.

"I'm tired of this. Let's finish," Officer Banks ordered.

Husky guy shoved Griff toward Banks, who swung, but Griff caught his arm. The men tumbled to the floor, beyond her sight. Ciara grabbed whatever weapon she could find, a can of shaving cream, and sneaked into Griff's bedroom. Luckily, he was on the ground floor.

She opened the window.

"Hey!" the husky guy said, coming at her.

She sprayed shaving cream into his eyes, tumbled out the window and ran like hell across the parking lot.

Her brain started processing. She had no phone, no wallet, no money. She couldn't trust the police, couldn't trust anyone. But needed help.

Adele was the only person Ciara could trust. She'd get to the museum, borrow some money from Adele and—and then what?

Someone grabbed her shoulder and yanked her back against his hard chest. The wind knocked from her lungs.

"How did they find us?" Griffin whispered against her ear. *"How?"*

Unable to speak, she shook her head.

He spun her around to face him. His cheek was bruised and his lip swollen. "You contacted them, didn't you?"

She blinked, tears burning her eyes. "I thought you were going to kill me, so I called the police."

"The police can't help you, Ciara. No one can."

Gripping her upper arm, he pulled her back to his apartment and shoved her through the window where she fell on top of the unconscious husky guy. She jumped off of him and spotted a gun on the floor.

"No!" She scooted away from the weapon.

Griff locked the window and pulled her to her feet, dragging her through the apartment to the trashed living room. Officer Banks lay unconscious on the floor.

"Is he…did you…" she stuttered, staring at the man's lifeless body.

In the back of her mind she registered the sound of Griffin shoving things into a bag.

"I've been compromised," he said.

She knew he wasn't speaking to her.

"When? I'll take care of it. Send a cleaner to the Bellevue apartment."

When he reached for her she instinctively tore off down the hallway, away from the violence, the blood, the broken furniture. Had to get away and find her safe life again.

A door slammed behind her followed by pounding footsteps. What was she thinking? She'd never outrun the bastard. But she had to try.

She pushed through the glass door into the Seattle rain and searched frantically for a person to signal. Someone to get help.

A woman was unbuckling a baby from the backseat of her car. Ciara couldn't utter a sound for fear of putting them in danger.

"Hey, wait up," Griffin said, with uncharacteristic

warmth to his voice. He put his arm around her shoulder, making her feel incredibly small and helpless. She wanted away from this man, but not enough to risk the baby's life.

Leading her to his car, he opened the passenger door and whispered against her ear, "Don't ever run from me again."

He slammed the door and paced around the front of the car, his eyes burning fire at her. She snapped her gaze from his and focused on her trembling fingers, folded in her lap.

Getting behind the wheel, he shoved the car in gear. "We need to get back to the museum. A package was delivered this morning. Go in and tell your old lady friend you're going away for the weekend with me. Bring the package with you."

"Where are we going?"

He didn't answer. Which meant what? He was going to kill her? She had to get help, alert Adele that her life was in danger.

"I wouldn't involve the old lady in this, if I were you. Things could turn out badly for her."

She couldn't believe he'd read her thoughts. Of course he did, he was an expert at emotional warfare.

They pulled into the museum parking lot, and Ciara opened her door.

"You have five minutes," he said.

She slammed the door and went inside. Griffin just wanted the package, that's all. Then he'd let her go, right? Go where? Where would she be safe?

Ciara went to her office and found Adele poised over a package with a letter opener in her hand.

"Hi, Adele."

The old woman jumped. "Oh my, I didn't expect you this morning. Are you all right? Did you recover from last night's excitement?"

"Yeah, I'm fine, but I can't stay and I need to ask a huge favor."

"Anything." She walked around the desk and touched Ciara's shoulder.

"Was wondering if you could run things this weekend. Griffin explained the misunderstanding about Aunt Miriam and he kept watch over me last night. We're going to get away for a few days."

"Oh my, Mr. Blue Eyes is that good, is he?"

"Good doesn't even come close."

Adele clapped her hands and hugged Ciara. "Wonderful, wonderful. I'm sorry you'll miss the birthday celebration."

Ciara stepped back. "Oh, right, sorry about that."

"Anything for romance."

"Yes, well, Mr. Romance is waiting outside. By the way, did we receive anything this morning?"

"One package, why?" She motioned to the box on the desk.

"You know me, can't resist checking it out." Ciara picked up the box. "Oh, and could you grab me an American Girl Mia doll for Griffin's daughter?"

"Of course, wait here." She winked.

Adele disappeared around the corner and Ciara placed this morning's delivery in a shopping bag. A few minutes later Adele returned and Ciara put the Mia doll in the bag, as well.

"You sure you'll be okay?" Ciara said.

"Don't worry about me or the museum. But I did

have one question. I was clearing some things out and found this key." She plucked a silver key from her pocket. "Do you know what it opens?"

"Huh. No."

"I found it on one of your grandmother's old key rings."

Ciara took it from Adele and analyzed it. "Odd."

"At any rate, you enjoy yourself." Adele gave Ciara a warm, loving hug, and Ciara nearly burst into tears. This woman was her only family, and Ciara didn't want to put her in danger.

"Thanks," Ciara said. "For everything."

"Go, go. Have fun."

When Ciara got outside, Griffin was headed toward her. "I'm coming, I'm coming." She got into the car and shut the door.

He got in beside her. "Did you get the package?"

She handed him the bag. "Today's delivery plus a Tonner doll for your daughter. If you even have a daughter. And forget the discount." She couldn't believe she'd just said that.

"What did you tell the old lady?"

"That we're off on a romantic weekend." She shot him a fake smile.

She noticed blood seeping form his lip and she fought back the urge to wipe it with something. *Idiot, he wants to kill you.*

"You should do something about your lip," she said, staring out the front window.

Ignoring her, he pulled out of the lot and headed for the freeway.

"Here." He grabbed her purse from the backseat. "I thought you'd need this."

She eyed him. "You're being nice to me? Why?"

"I was hoping we could work together. Whatever they're paying you, the U.S. government will pay more if you help us shut down the smuggling operation."

"Yeah, well, would love to help, but like I've said a million times, I don't know anything about smuggling."

"Right. Give me the key."

"What?"

"The key the old lady gave you."

"How did you know about that? God, you bugged me or something?" She took off her coat.

"Stop it. Just give it to me."

She placed it in his palm and turned to focus out the window. She wanted so desperately to rid herself of this bully.

Half an hour later he pulled into a hotel just north of Seattle. He led her into a room.

"Go sit down," he ordered.

She sat beside the table and crossed her arms over her chest.

Using his knife, Griffin sliced open the box and pulled out a doll in plastic wrap. Ciara didn't remember ordering this one either. A sick feeling settled in her chest.

Griff removed the plastic and scanned the doll with the small device.

"Nothing." He pocketed the device and looked at her. "This is getting tedious."

"Is that the word for it?" She snatched the doll from him.

He opened his laptop, connected a mini-scanner to it and placed the key on the scanner.

"So, this is where you store the contraband?"

She glanced at the screen. It showed a Web site for a storage facility in Everett.

"I didn't know—"

"Save it. Let's go."

IT WAS wearing on him. Her innocent act, the tears, the fear he read in her green eyes every time he was abrupt with her. She was terrified of him. Good, she should be. He was the one who was going to put her out of business and lock her up for life.

He focused on that goal and shoved aside the nagging sensation at the base of his neck. Something didn't fit, but he couldn't place it. Not yet.

As he went through his fifth storage box, this one filled with china plates wrapped in newspaper, Ciara kept repeating, "I never knew this place existed," as if he would believe her if she said it often enough. That's what was nagging at him: she was brainwashing him into believing her innocence.

She shook her head, sifting through a box of papers. "How could I not know about this?"

He spun on her. "Just stop, damn it."

"What?"

"The innocent victim act. You're wasting your breath."

"Apparently."

She went back to analyzing contents of a file box. "So, you're a government agent on a mission to find chips that I've smuggled? What kind of chips?"

"Microchips to give terrorists control of jet engines."

"Oh," she said, studying the document in her hands. "Ick."

"Yeah, ick. Didn't occur to you that your greed would cost lives?"

"Hey, guy, if I were making millions from smuggling, I'd be living in Medinah and driving a Lexus."

He went back to his box of wrapped china. "You wouldn't want to draw attention to yourself."

"And you are determined not to believe me."

"It's my job—"

"Look me straight in the eye and tell me you think I'm capable of smuggling weapons to kill people."

He couldn't look at her.

"Come on, you must have done background on me, right? What did it show? That I was a preschool teacher before taking over Gran's museum. I'm honest to a fault. I've never even gotten a speeding ticket, and you're accusing me of being a smuggler for terrorists? How ridiculous is that?"

"I'm assuming that's a rhetorical question?"

"Whatever." She went back to analyzing her box of paperwork.

He was tired of going through someone else's things, tired of being on the run with a woman who was so convincing about her innocence.

"What is this?" she whispered.

He went to her and read over her shoulder. It was the title and key to a house on Whidbey Island. Whidbey would be an ideal spot to dock a boat and unload goods unnoticed.

"She never told me she owned a house on Whidbey Island."

"She obviously never told you a lot of things."

"She wasn't a smuggler."

Her gut-wrenching protest made him wonder if she truly was an innocent drawn into this mess. Didn't have time to wonder.

His PDA beeped a text message:

Your apartment was empty.

Which meant the bastards had gotten away.

"Grab the title and keys to the Whidbey property," Griff said.

No reason to panic. The big dude and dirty cop couldn't have tracked them here.

The back of his neck pinched. Griff easily tagged her blouse with a listening device. Who's to say they hadn't done the same?

With one hand holding his Glock and the other gripping her arm, he flipped off the lights and cracked the door—

It swung open, knocking him in the face. Stunned, he stumbled back and the door slammed shut, plunging them into complete darkness.

Chapter Five

Damn, they were all going to die, hundreds, maybe thousands of people because Griff screwed up.

He slowed his breathing, stayed low and waited. If he couldn't see the bastard, then the bastard couldn't see Griff.

Ciara was unusually quiet. She'd stumbled backward when the door whipped open. Did she fall and hit her head? Couldn't think about that now.

The lights came on and Griff charged the husky guy, slamming him to the ground. Husky guy's gun discharged and Ciara screamed, the sound bouncing off the walls like a siren.

"You again," Griff said, pinning the guy and applying pressure to his wrist. The guy's fingers opened and the gun dropped to the ground. "How did you find us?"

"No!" she screamed.

Griff glanced up. The dirty cop fired and Griff used husky guy as a shield. The guy took a bullet in the shoulder.

"Idiot, you shot me!" he bellowed. The guy crawled to the wall and leaned against it. "Hell, that hurts."

"Sorry, Chuck. I won't miss this time." He aimed the gun…

…And was nailed in the head by a paperweight. Ciara screeched at the top of her lungs and she fired off one thing after another at the cop. He lunged toward her and Griff nailed him in the knees. They went down, the gun flying from the cop's hand. Griff knocked him out and glanced at Ciara, who had her foot on the husky guy's gun as he reached for it. She picked up the gun and aimed it at their attacker

"Ciara, don't," Griff said.

She backed up, pointing the gun at husky guy.

"Ciara," Griff said.

She spun and aimed the gun at Griff. He raised his hands. "You don't want to shoot me. Put it down."

"Why, so you can terrorize me some more? How about I lock you in here with these killers and you can all kill each other?"

She edged toward the door.

"I can't let you leave, you know that," Griff said.

"I won't let you hurt me anymore."

She fired the weapon and Griff hit the floor, but she intentionally missed, slammed the door and locked it.

"Open the door, Ciara!"

Nothing. Husky guy laughed.

"What's so funny? You're going to bleed to death," Griff shot over his shoulder. Husky guy stopped laughing.

Griff swiped his Glock from the floor and fired three shots at the lock. The door swung open and he spotted her sprint toward the main drag. Fine, he'd let her run until she was exhausted, then he'd catch her. He slashed two tires on their pursuers' SUV to slow them down.

He got behind the wheel of his car, pushing aside the thought that she'd fired the gun, but didn't shoot him. She could have. But didn't. Why?

She approached the road and waved wildly at cars passing by. Not good. She'd be hit or arrested and at this point Griff didn't need the complication.

He pulled up beside her and opened his window. "Get in the car."

She ignored him and stretched out her arms, waving for help. Her hair flew wildly about her face, her sleeve was ripped and her eyes radiated fear. The passers by probably thought she was an escapee from a mental ward.

He glanced in his rearview mirror and noticed dirty cop standing in the doorway to the storage unit. Great.

Griff got out of the car and picked her up, kicking and shouting. He plopped her into the passenger seat. "Stop or you're going in the trunk."

Glancing up, Griff spotted the dirty cop racing after them. Griff got into the car, put it in gear and sped off. Adrenaline pulsed through his body at the thought of nearly dying back there and failing his mission.

They drove in silence for a good twenty minutes. Griff tired to figure out where they would be safe, at least long enough for him to figure out his next move.

He glanced at Ciara. "Are you okay?"

"Sure, wonderful."

"Are you hurt, physically?"

She hugged her midsection and stared out the window, looking so damn fragile. Her enemies would keep coming until they got her again, terrorized her for information and when they were through, kill her.

Griff shouldn't care.

Too many things plagued his common sense, too many signs that she didn't, in fact, know what the hell was going on. She'd been caught in the middle.

And the bastards were going to catch her because

they were tracking the two of them. There was only one way Banks and Husky could be doing that.

Griff squeezed the steering wheel. She wouldn't like it, but he knew what had to be done.

He pulled off the highway and parked in a wooded area. He grabbed an undershirt from his overnight bag in the trunk and opened Ciara's door.

"Come on." He offered his hand. She ignored it and got out of the car.

"Let's walk a bit," he said.

With wide green eyes, she placed her hand to the charm at her neck. "You're going to shoot me...out here in this beautiful place?"

"I am not going to shoot you."

He took her hand, hoping he wouldn't have to pull her like a stubborn mule. Surprisingly, she followed without much protest. They started down a trail surrounded by evergreens and cedars, as he considered the possibility he was holding the hand of an innocent.

She'd saved his life back there. The dirty cop was about to shoot him, but Ciara distracted Banks by hurling odds and ends from her grandmother's storage boxes. A criminal would have let him die.

She'd seemed genuinely surprised when she'd discovered the vacation property her grandmother owned on Whidbey. Okay, so maybe Ciara wasn't a smuggler, yet granny surely was. Coming to grips with that fact wasn't going to be easy for her.

Once they were deep into the woods, he stopped and turned to her. "I need you to take off your clothes."

She backed up.

"Please, Ciara, I think something's been planted on your clothing that's allowing them to track us."

She blinked, gripping her sweater closed in front.

"I've got an undershirt that will cover you and you can wear my jacket."

But she didn't move.

He took a step toward her, then another. If he didn't know better, he'd think her in shock with her eyes focused straight ahead at nothing.

"If you don't take off your clothes, they'll catch up to us again. You don't want that, do you?"

She shook her head, but gripped her sweater tighter.

Damn, he was going to have to do this for her. Gently, he placed his hands over hers, stroked the backs of her knuckles with his thumbs.

"It's okay," he said. "I'm not going to hurt you anymore."

He uncurled her fingers from the cotton sweater and lowered her hands to her sides. Holding them for a second, he hoped the connection might comfort her.

Who was he kidding? He'd just spent the last twelve-plus hours terrorizing her.

He unbuttoned her top sweater button, then the second button. She closed her eyes. What the hell, did she think he was going to force himself on her?

Griff steadied her chin between his forefinger and thumb. "Look at me, Ciara."

Fear tinged her striking green eyes. Fear and determination. Good, she was going to need lots of that to stay alive.

"Look, your grandmother's smuggling has gotten you into a load of trouble. You need to take off everything but your underwear so they can't track us. Are you up to it or shall I do it for you?"

She snapped her chin away. "I'll do it."

Good, he'd hoped his accusation about her grandmother would snap her out of it.

Holding his gaze, she unbuttoned her blouse and handed it to him, then unzipped her pants and stepped out of them. Leaning against the tree, she took off her shoes and socks. There was nothing left but her delicate lace bra and panties, and her defiant glare.

She was challenging him to touch her, but he wouldn't, not now, not ever. Not like that. There was no place in Griff's life for anything beyond recreational affairs, and this woman was way too grounded to play at recreation.

Which was another thing that worried him: she was one of those loyal-to-a-fault creatures, the kind that could rouse his dormant conscience. He couldn't risk that.

She snatched the undershirt from his hand and slipped it on. Searching her clothes, he found a small metal disc stuck to the back of her shirt collar. His fingers twitched at the thought of one of those bastards getting close enough to touch her shirt.

Then he picked up her sweater and felt a hard square device in her pocket. Pulling it out, he recognized a beeper that doubled as a jamming mechanism. "Where did you get this?"

"I found it last night when I was closing."

Made sense. The device would block the security code, shutting down the system and allowing the terrorists to get into the museum, but she'd accidentally taken it with her and ruined their plan.

Removing the battery, Griff pocketed it thinking he could have it traced to the source, giving him another lead on who they were dealing with.

He tossed her clothes to the ground, leaving the

tracking device to draw the goons here, into the middle of the woods. Maybe if they found her clothes they'd think she'd been a victim of foul play and would stop looking for her.

Dream on, Griff.

Ciara brushed past him and stormed back up the trail toward the car. What a mess. No other word to describe it. She was an innocent dragged into this conspiracy to kill Americans. Whether or not her grandmother played a part in the smuggling Ciara had been tagged by both sides: the terrorists wanted the chips and the NSA wanted to stop delivery.

The only thing Griff had to go on was a mysterious property owned by the grandmother. Maybe if he confided in Ciara, shared some of the information they'd unearthed about the smuggling she'd help him put it together, find the missing pieces that would lead them to the hand-off.

His cell vibrated.

"Black," he said.

"Status?"

Ciara stepped on something and cried out in pain. "Damn it, fickle, fickle, fickle."

He cupped her elbow for support. She glared at him and wrenched away, hobbling ahead.

"I've found property owned by the grandmother up north," Griff said to his commanding officer. "We're checking it out as a possible drop location."

"We?"

"Me and the girl."

"The smuggler?"

"There's a definite possibility she's an innocent, sir."

"Then she's excess baggage."

"She might be able to help."

"Or mess things up. You know the danger of involving innocents."

"Yes, sir."

"Keep me posted."

Griff didn't need to be reminded about involving innocents in this business. The image of his fiancée, Mary, lying unconscious in the hospital bed crossed his thoughts. They couldn't prove the accident was related to his work, but the possibility gutted him just the same. He'd worked so hard to keep her safe, keep her at a distance so his enemies wouldn't find her.

After Mary's accident Griffin Black was born. A new identity, a new life and complete anonymity with help from the agency that owned him. They orchestrated the accident that officially killed him and he never looked back. Couldn't. He'd hardened his soul to anything resembling love or compassion and focused on doing his job.

He thought about what lack of focus could do to an agent and those depending on him to save their lives. Agent Dalton Keen had nearly lost his life and that of a rescued hostage, because he'd trusted an endearing female informant who'd ended up being a spy.

Ciara approached the car. She was also endearing, gentle and so damn authentic. That must have been how she'd cracked the protective shell encasing his heart, making him care about what happened to her. Caring about her would put both their lives at risk.

She climbed into the car and he considered his next move. He'd have to stop and buy her clothes, no way around it. He hoped she didn't bolt when he went into the store. He could cuff her to the steering wheel but knew that wouldn't go over well. Tough, he couldn't risk losing her.

He got into the car.

"What size are you?" He searched his GPS for a nearby Target store.

"Why?"

"I'm going to buy you clothes."

"No, I mean, why is this happening?"

He glanced at her, then snapped his gaze back to the navigational device. He couldn't look too long into those sad eyes, tinged with confusion.

Things were going to get even more confusing. This charming, innocent young woman could very well be on the run indefinitely.

He knew the feeling. Hadn't he been running for the past seven years? Only, he chose to run. Ciara had been forced into a state of constant paranoia never knowing from which direction the next assault would come.

"You're involved in this because someone's been smuggling contraband through the doll museum," he said.

"Someone? So you admit it's not me?"

"It looks that way."

"And you think it was Gran?"

"Yes."

"Why would she do that?"

"Money."

She stared out the window. "But she never had any."

"She needed to make it look that way. We'll visit the property to see if the dolls were sent there."

"Property I didn't even know about." She studied her fingers.

Something twisted in his chest. He could put up all the walls he wanted, but Ciara had a way of edging her way inside, settling there and making Griff need to protect her.

Focus.

It was a struggle to focus with her beside him. What made her different from the others?

It didn't matter. He had to get what information he could and dump her as quickly as possible. It would help to think of her the way his CO did: as excess baggage.

THE MAN confused the hell out of her. One minute he was asking if she was okay, the next he was handcuffing her to the steering wheel. She eyed her wrist, encased in cold metal. Jerk. He may believe she wasn't a smuggler, but he didn't trust her not to run away.

She shivered. She understood she needed to take off her clothes in order to prevent the bad guys from tracking them, but he'd found the tracking device. Why couldn't she have just put her clothes back on? Did he get a charge out of seeing her in her underwear?

You'd never know by the look on his face. Anger lit those blue eyes of his, eyes she once thought magnetic. Now they just scared her. There was something behind those eyes that made her want to squeeze her hand from the cuffs and run, even when all she wore was a man's undershirt, a bra and panties.

She tugged on her wrist. Nope, she wasn't going anywhere. Maybe that was a good thing. Griff may not be her ally, but at least she knew he was resourceful enough to keep them both from getting killed. If she stuck close to him she'd stay alive, at least until she could...what? Disappear? She wasn't one to run from things. Gran had taught her to stand up for what she believed in, and right now she believed in Gran's innocence. But how could she prove it?

By doing an investigation of her own. The sooner

she got answers, the sooner they'd resolve this disaster and Griff would be out of her life and take his violence with him.

Stretching, she dug into her purse and found her cell phone. It had little battery left, so she'd have to make this a quick call. She dialed the museum.

"Ruth's Doll Emporium," Adele answered.

"Adele, it's Ciara."

"Oh my God, child, where are you? I've been frantic."

"What's wrong?"

"Shortly after you left federal officers came by asking about you. They looked very serious. What's going on?"

"I'm not sure, but—"

"And that witch Lucinda has been calling every fifteen minutes, demanding I give her your cell phone number, but I didn't want her to interrupt your romantic interlude with Mr. Blue Eyes."

"Thanks, I—"

"Just tell me you're okay."

Ciara hesitated. "I'm fine, but I need a favor. Do you know about a property on Whidbey that Gran owned?"

"Oh, fiddle, how would Ruth be able to afford property up there?"

"I don't know, but I found a deed in her name."

"You don't say."

The phone line clicked.

"Hang on, it's probably Lucinda again," Adele said.

The line went silent. Ciara glanced over her shoulder at the store. Griff was nowhere in sight.

"I'm back," Adele said in a frantic tone. "That witch is going to drive me to gamble."

"Go ahead and give her my cell if that will get her off your back."

"I'm worried about your back. Why are federal agents looking for you?"

"Maybe because they think Gran has been smuggling things through doll acquisitions."

"Ruthie? Sweet Ruthie?"

"Don't worry, I'm going to prove her innocence. I need Pete, the computer geek's cell phone number. Can you find it for me?"

"Sure, hang on."

Suddenly the door swung open and Griff snatched the phone from her hand.

"What the hell are you doing?" he demanded.

She automatically ducked, thinking he might hit her he looked so furious.

"If you'll stop freaking out, I'll tell you," she shot back. She was tired of being afraid of him, afraid and defenseless.

"No one can help you, Ciara. You got that?"

"Stop being a bully and listen to me."

"Shut up, just don't say another word."

He slammed her door. She seethed. Here she was trying to help him and he completely distrusted her.

Fine. She'd let him have it, tell him that although his goal was to nail the mystery smugglers, hers was to clear Gran's name. If they worked together and trusted each other, they'd both get what they needed.

He got into the car, shoved a shopping bag into the backseat and uncuffed her.

"You can dress later," he snapped.

"I'm trying to help here."

"What, by involving the cops?"

"I didn't call the cops."

"No?" He motioned out the front window. Two security cars flanked Griff's car and an officer got out.

Griff glared at her. "I told you, Ciara, I'm the only one who can save your life."

The security guard walked up to her window, eyed her, then motioned for his partner.

"Sonofabitch," Griff swore.

The second guard knocked on his window and Griff lowered it.

"Sir, I'm going to have to ask you get out of the car."

Chapter Six

Even Ciara knew the danger of this complication. If security alerted the local cops and they took Griff in for questioning, he couldn't find the microchips and they'd end up in a plane, killing hundreds, possibly thousands.

If his story was even true.

It was so dang crazy, it had to be true. Not only would hundreds of lives be at risk, but also where would that leave Ciara? Heading back to Bellevue where the thugs, federal agents and who knows who else would be waiting for her.

Like it or not, Griffin Black was her best option for staying alive.

Her car door opened and a young, redheaded guard smiled down at her. "Ma'am, you all right?"

"I'm—"

Griff spread his hands across the hood of his car as the cop searched him for weapons. Oh God, they were going to find something, call the local cops, complicating this situation even further.

"I'm fine," she said, getting out of the car. "We went to the park and I'm such a klutz, I fell into the lake and ruined my clothes and luckily Griff had a spare undershirt and I couldn't go into Target dressed like this, so he went in to buy me clothes. What a sweetie, huh?" She hoped some of her rambling sounded believable.

"See?" She reached into the car and pulled out the bag of clothes.

"We got a call from some shoppers saying this man was abusing you."

"Oh, that." *Think fast, girl.* "It's silly, really, but," she pulled out a lime-green blouse from the bag. "Tell me the truth, does this look even remotely good on me? It's not my color." She held the blouse to her chin and tipped her head to the side.

The redheaded guard glanced at his partner, then back to Ciara. She didn't miss the quizzical look on Griff's face.

"So, he wasn't hurting you?" Red asked.

"Yeah, he was hurting my pride. Neon green. Honest to Pete, who on earth would think to buy that color for a redhead like me?" She smiled, a warm, friendly smile, hoping they'd drop it.

"I'm sorry for the confusion, Officer." Even though Griff spoke to the guard, he held her gaze. His blue eyes weren't dark like before, his expression had softened.

Was he…thankful for her storytelling?

The redheaded guard searched her face. "You're sure you're okay? You don't feel threatened by this man?"

She forced a smile. "Not at all. But thanks for your concern."

Red nodded. "Have a nice evening."

"Thanks, you, too."

The guards drove off and Ciara glanced at Griff.

"Get in the car." He got behind the wheel and waited.

What was his problem?

She climbed in and buckled up, holding the bag of clothes in her lap.

But they didn't move. She glanced at him. "I thought we were in a hurry."

"What was that about?"

"What?"

He leveled her with a scolding glare. "That story about falling into the lake."

"I thought it was pretty good."

"What compelled you to come up with a ridiculous story like that?"

"I didn't want you to be taken in for questioning. Was I wrong? I mean, you need to find the microchips, right?"

He snapped his gaze from hers and wrapped his fingers around the steering wheel. "I can take care of myself," he said.

"Okay, great. I'll remember that next time and let them lock you up."

"Who was on the phone?"

"Adele."

He shoved the car in gear and pulled out of the lot. "Why did you call her?"

"Because, believe it or not, I'm trying to help you. I asked her for the phone number of our computer geek. I'd hoped to call him and set up a password so I could access the museum computer from a remote site, thinking maybe I could look for abnormalities. Unfortunately my phone was taken away."

"My agency can access your computer."

"Oh, well, I didn't know that, did I?" She squared off at him. "I want this whole nightmare to end. Tell me how I can make that happen."

"You can't."

"Bull. It's my museum you're accusing of being part of a smuggling operation. I need to help. I need to clear Gran's name."

"That kind of naive thinking will get you killed."

"And your cynicism will blow up your head." Dumb, but she said the first thing that came to mind.

He raised an eyebrow. "Blow up my head?"

"Whatever. What can I do to help?"

He focused on the freeway ramp. "Just keep quiet and let me think."

ONCE safely on the ferry, Griff got out of the car and let Ciara dress in private. Leaning against the car, he eyed Puget Sound, wondering if the terrorist agents had discovered Granny's hideaway.

No. Griff had taken the only documentation regarding the property on Whidbey, and even if they knew about it, it would take time to tend to the big guy's bullet wound and fix their car.

Griff took a deep breath, filling his lungs with fresh Pacific Northwest air. He was still trying to figure out how a simple assignment had become so complicated. *Find the chip in a doll's eye in a specific museum* had turned into finding three chips in undisclosed locations.

More variables he couldn't control.

Any more than he could control his protective feelings for Ciara. He shoved the thought aside. If he cared at all for the fragile creature he'd keep his perspective and shut down any and all romantic stirrings for her. He *wasn't* exactly boyfriend material.

The car door opened.

"How do I look?" she said, dressed in the stretch pants, T-shirt and blouse he'd bought her.

"Good enough."

"Gee, thanks." She eyed her reflection in the side mirror. "Don't suppose you thought to pick up some makeup." She glanced at him. "Never mind."

The thought didn't occur to him because he didn't realize she wore any. Ciara looked nothing like the females he'd dated, if you could call it dating. He went for the high-maintenance, glamorous ones because they somehow made him feel better about himself. Shallow bastard.

"We can stop at a grocery store on the way to the cabin," he said.

"Goodie."

"A brief stop. We need to get to the Whidbey property as soon as possible."

"And then?"

"Hope the contraband has been delivered there."

"Gran's been dead for six months. She couldn't have been involved. I'll bet they're using her name as a cover, that she didn't even know about the Whidbey property."

"The deed and keys were in her storage unit."

"To make her look guilty and protect the real criminal."

"She could have been working with a partner," Griff said.

"You just won't give up, will you?"

"We intercepted e-mails sent and received from your e-mail address. Our best suspects are employees of the museum, and more likely, its owners."

"If you'd let me call my computer guy I could have him check on the account activity."

"I'll need to do background on him first." He retrieved his laptop from the car. "What's his name?"

"Pete Desai. Lives in Seattle. Does all kinds of free-lance stuff. He was referred to us by Lucinda."

"And Lucinda is?"

"One of our benefactors. She donates some amazing collectible dolls to the museum."

"Lucinda's last name and where she lives?"

"You're kidding."

He couldn't believe her loyalty to friends, especially to friends who were putting her in danger.

"Give it up," he said.

Narrowing her eyes, she said, "Lucinda Brooks. Kirkland, Washington."

"Great." He sent an e-mail to his IT contact in D.C., then put his laptop to sleep. "Should know in an hour or so. You hungry? They've got food up top."

She crossed her arms over her chest and eyed him.

"What?"

"You're not a bad guy when you're being polite."

"Oh, I'm bad, Ciara. Trust me on that one. Come on, let's get something to eat."

SHE STUDIED him as he led her upstairs to the snack bar. Griff missed nothing, as his eyes calculated each and every person they passed. She couldn't imagine what it must be like to have to live in such a constant state of alertness, bordering on aggression.

He motioned for her to lead them into the snack bar where her nostrils flared at the scent of cheeseburgers and clam chowder. The chowder reminded her of Gran and their trips into the city where they'd wander Seattle's waterfront. They hadn't done it often, so it was a treat to get out of the suburbs into the heart of the city.

She got her chowder and stood in line. Griff stood behind her carrying nothing.

"You're not eating?"

"Not hungry."

"Eat anyway. Go on, grab a cheeseburger."

He narrowed his eyes as if offended by her bossy tone.

"Please? I hate eating alone."

He grabbed a cheeseburger and bottle of water and insisted on paying. It's the least he could do, she mused, going over the events of the past twenty-four hours. A part of her was still in shock, unable to process that less than a year ago she was a preschool teacher whose biggest daily concerns were runny noses and boo-boos, and today she was fighting to stay alive.

Her stomach tightened. Did no good to obsess over the life-threatening situation.

They sat at a table in the corner. Griff continued to scan the passengers as they ambled past.

"Do you ever relax?" she asked.

"Eat your chowder."

"Or answer a question directly?"

"No."

"Ooo, you did it, I'm impressed."

"You talk a lot."

"Tend do to that when I'm nervous."

"You're safe. For the moment."

"Pardon me if I don't completely believe that. I mean, I figured we were safe at the storage unit and then at the store parking lot."

"That's why I never relax. I never know what's coming next."

"Stressful. I could so not live that way." She stopped eating, suddenly aware of her situation.

"What's wrong?" he asked.

"I just realized I might not have much longer to live." She studied him. "That's accurate, isn't it?"

He glanced at a couple passing by. "Don't think about it. With any luck we'll close this one and you can get back to your life."

"Running a doll museum under investigation for smuggling." She leaned back. "They'll have to shut us down."

He didn't respond, which she took as an affirmation of her suspicions.

"Great, time to find yet another career."

"You were a preschool teacher. Couldn't you go back to that?"

"Maybe." She stirred her soup. "I loved being around the kids. They're so honest and pure. What you see is what you get. Know what I mean?"

"I guess."

She suspected he didn't.

"But," she continued, "running Gran's business sparked something inside of me. I like being a manager, troubleshooting business challenges, making customers happy. What about you? What made you go into this line of work?" She wanted to distract herself, to think about something other than starting over again.

"I was in Special Ops. When I finished my tour I was offered a position with the NSA."

"As a secret agent?"

"They don't call us that."

"Then what do they call you?"

"Nonexistent."

"That doesn't sound like much fun."

"Someone has to do it."

"Why does it have to be you?"

"Because I'm good at it. Besides, it has its perks."

"Yeah? Like what?"

"I get to see the world. I'm not tied down by a boring job or demanding family."

"That's two. Keep going and maybe you'll convince me you love your work."

She couldn't help herself. There was something in his tone that made her think he was definitely not at peace with what he did.

"Why is everything a fight with you?" he asked.

"I'm not fighting. I'm trying to keep this stimulating conversation going so I don't have to sit with my thoughts and panic about my tenuous future."

He held her gaze with those fantastic blue eyes of his. "I'll do my best to keep you safe."

"Yeah, well, that's great for the next few days, but what about for the rest of my life?"

GRIFF HADN'T a clue how to respond, so he didn't. They got back into the car and deboarded the ferry. A few minutes later Ciara fell asleep, allowing him to relax.

Her incessant chatter and questions made him edgy, probably because they forced him to think about things usually outside of his scope.

Truth was, the rest of someone's life had never crossed Griff's mind. Life only stretched as far as his next assignment and keeping the country safe from crazy bastards on power trips.

Yet lately he had been thinking a little further out, even caught himself wondering what he'd be doing fifteen or twenty years down the road. He'd be too old for this kind of work. Surely the government would give him another assignment.

Like a desk job. A sardonic smile curled his lips. He'd rather take an assignment in a third world country before being jailed in an office. Griff needed the diversity of doing something different every few weeks. Being strapped to a desk would kill him from the inside out.

He eyed his passenger. A few strands of flaming red hair slanted across her face and he gently brushed them aside. He had to admire her loyalty to her grandmother, even though the evidence pointed to the old woman as a co-conspirator. He wondered if her death had, in fact, been from natural causes, or if her partner had orchestrated it because Granny didn't follow orders, or maybe even wanted out?

Time to call back east and have Granny's medicals checked out. Just in case. If they could track visitors to the hospital they might be able to expose her partner.

One thing for sure, Ciara was an innocent. Which meant if he had any sense, he'd dump her ASAP.

He'd call Dalton Keen and see if the agent had space to house Ciara until this case was resolved. Griff pictured the handsome Dalton welcoming Ciara into his temporary quarters with his charming smile and wounded hero act. Women loved to heal a wounded soul—at least that was Griff's experience.

Griff rolled tension from his neck. What the hell did he care if Dalton and Ciara hit it off?

They approached the town of Langley and he slowed to the thirty-five-mile speed limit. Didn't want to attract attention.

He glanced at his navigational device. He'd turned off the sound so that it wouldn't wake up Ciara with its direction.

Again he was thinking too much about her comfort.

But then she'd saved his butt and more than once.

Sure she did, Black. You're her only hope of seeing her thirtieth birthday.

He'd read her file. She'd turned twenty-nine last month. So damn young. Or maybe it was her sheltered life that made her seem so young and made Griff feel ancient at thirty-four.

He followed the GPS's directions, turned onto a dirt road and continued another few minutes before spotting a log cabin in the distance. Interesting. He'd never pegged a granny-type owning a rustic home.

In the twilight he eyed the well-tended property: the lawn was neatly trimmed and flower boxes overflowed with color. Pulling up the drive, he noticed a soft glow shine through the open window of the cabin. He parked behind a tree and got out, scanning the property and planning his next move.

"What is it?" Ciara said, her voice hoarse from sleep as she got out of the car and spotted the cabin. "Wow."

"Looks like someone's inside. I'm going to check it out. You stay here."

She nodded, eyes wide. She was probably flashing back to the multiple times she'd been brutalized in the past twenty-four hours.

"Get in the car and lock the doors until I get back," he ordered.

"What if you don't come back?"

Not likely, but he read the panic in her eyes. He pulled a business card from his wallet, scanned his phone and found the contact information for Dalton Keen. He scribbled the number on the card and handed it to her.

"This is another agent over in Port Townsend. If anything happens to me, contact him. He'll know what to do."

She nodded.

"I'll leave the keys in the car."

She studied the business card.

"Ciara?"

She glanced up.

"I'll be right back."

He shut the car door on her lost expression and started for the house, keeping to the cover of trees and shrubs. It was so quiet you could hear the water splash against the shoreline. But he heard nothing else, no sound of life inside the cabin.

Glock in his hand, he rushed to the house and edged his way to the side window. He peered inside the main room, dimly lit by a lamp in the corner.

The place looked immaculate and ready for its next renter. A blanket was neatly folded and stretched across the back of the sofa, and four place settings, complete with wineglasses, were set on the wood dining table. It reminded him of a scene from a Martha Stewart show on how to entertain friends in your country home.

Someone managed the property, but luckily no one was inside at present. He spied a timer attached to the outlet where the lamp was plugged in. Probably set up to keep prowlers away.

Using the key they'd found in the storage unit, he let himself in and did a thorough search. The house was empty. Griff went back to the car.

"It's safe," he said, pulling the car closer to the house.

"But the light?" Ciara asked.

"The light is on a timer, probably set up by whoever is managing the property. Let's go inside."

"You sure it's okay?"

"Your grandmother owned the property. Technically you should have inherited it upon her death."

"It wasn't in her will."

"The paperwork was dated eight months ago. She probably didn't have time to update her will. We should be safe for the night at least."

Ciara nodded, but didn't look convinced.

"Come on, we'll go inside and find the management company's contact information."

Grabbing her purse and bag of clothes, she opened the car door. He offered his hand again, and this time she took it, slipping her petite fingers into his palm. The warmth shot straight to the barrier around his heart.

Yes, he would have to leave her with Dalton Keen for her own good. If her touch had this kind of effect on him, it would dull his instincts, putting her life in even greater danger.

He opened the door and motioned for her to enter. He glanced across the property, then followed her inside.

"Wow," she hushed. "It's nice."

She set her bag of clothes on a reclining chair and walked across the twenty-foot living room to the picture window overlooking Puget Sound. Hugging herself, she rubbed her arms and said, "It's so peaceful here."

It was only temporary peace. But he didn't have the heart to say it out loud.

"I'll build a fire," he offered.

"That would be great. I need to find the bathroom."

He opened the wood stove and lit a match to prime the flue.

A screech echoed down the hall. Griff was across the room in seconds, holding her in his arms.

"What is it?"

"Outside.... Someone's outside."

Chapter Seven

"Turn off the light," he ordered, pulling out his gun.

Ciara raced to the corner and unplugged the lamp, her fingers trembling. Just when she thought they were safe and could rest easy for a few hours, everything sped up again. Griff didn't seem bothered by the prowler, who could very well be one of the terrorists assigned to find the chip—or Ciara. Or both.

But how could they have been tracked when she'd left her clothes and the tracking device behind in the woods?

"What do you—"

Griff silenced her with a forefinger to his lips. "Get behind the sofa and stay there."

She crawled behind the overstuffed denim sofa, hugging her knees to her chest. She was beginning to resent this feeling of helplessness, of being victimized.

Yet Griff seemed energized by it, almost like he got a charge out of danger and the threat of death.

She involuntarily shuddered, then heard the door open and close. Rats. Griff went outside, leaving her alone in the cabin. If anything happened to him, she was screwed.

The image of Griff repeatedly defending her against

her attackers shot to the forefront of her mind. She shouldn't worry. He was a trained warrior, intent on protecting her.

Because you have something he wants, Ciara, you're his only lead to finding the microchips.

Moonlight streamed through the picture window as she hovered beside the couch. Now she really wished she had signed up for the self-defense class that Adele's daughter had taken last spring. But then, as Adele said, her daughter lived in a dangerous city neighborhood, not in a safe suburb.

A squeak echoed from the side window. Someone was trying to break in. She curled up against the sofa and buried her face against folded arms.

Breathe.

She heard another squeak followed by a thud.

"Crap," a male voice swore. Not Griff's. She fisted her hands, frustrated that all she could do was hide in the corner instead of defending herself.

She was tired of being a victim. With a deep breath, she rushed toward the kitchen, pulled open a cabinet and grabbed the first weapon she got her hands on: the glass top to a blender.

"Who the hell are you?" a man accused, towering over the counter and peering down at her. He was young, maybe twenty, with long brown hair and a nose ring.

"Get back or I'll smash your brains!" she cried, jumping to her feet and winding up with the appliance.

"Drop your weapon," Griff said from behind the intruder.

"Yeah, drop it," the kid said.

"I meant you." Griff leaned into the kid's back, pinning him against the counter opposite Ciara.

"Me? I've got nothing, well, except for the Swiss Army knife I use to open beer bottles."

"Spread 'em," Griff ordered.

The kid spread his arms across the counter as Griff searched him for weapons.

"Hey, what about her? She was going to bash my brains in with a blender."

She slipped the blender to the counter and sighed.

Griff glanced over the kid's shoulder at her. "You okay?"

"Great, yeah, sure."

She turned on the faucet and splashed cool water on her face. It wasn't until that moment that she realized her cheeks were burning red-hot.

"Okay, kid, who are you?" Griff spun the punk around and pointed a gun at his chest."

With arms raised he said, "Whoa, relax man, cool it. I'm T.J. My dad owns Crate & Munster Real Estate. They manage this place."

"And you're here why?"

Ciara flipped on the kitchen light and came around the bar to study the boy. He had a sweet face, a slight beard growth on his chin and tattoos climbing up his neck.

"I... Well, my dad asked me to check up on the cottage."

"Uh-huh." Griff holstered his gun.

"What?" The kid smirked and lowered his hands.

"And your buddies in the SUV out there, your dad asked them to help you check on the cottage?"

Ciara went to the front window and spotted the vehicle. Someone honked the horn, then two guys got out. One of them put out his hands as if to say, *well?*

"We were on our way to a party and I told dad I'd stop by and check up on things," T.J. explained.

"Why did you leave your booze outside on the porch?" The kid shrugged.

"Come on, kid. You were planning to have your party here because you knew it was vacant, right?"

"No," he said, in a defiant tone. "Who the hell are you anyway? And why the piece?"

"I'm a federal officer," Griff said.

"And I own this place." Ciara walked up to him.

"Bull. A nice old lady owns it."

"My grandmother died, so it's mine."

"Oh, no wonder I haven't seen her around."

"Give me your father's phone number," Griff said.

"Why? You're not going to narc on me, are you? Come on, man, you remember what it was like to be a teenager, right? I mean, he's going to kill me if he finds out I was here."

"I'll make you a deal. I won't bust you if you keep quiet about finding us."

"You want privacy, I get it." He quirked his eyebrow.

Ciara nearly corrected him, but held her tongue. Thinking Griff and Ciara needed a weekend of hot sex might appeal to the kid and earn his loyalty.

"I'll call your dad and let him know we're here. And I need a favor." Griff slipped a fifty-dollar bill from his wallet, then pulled a piece of paper from his pocket. He ripped off a bit of paper and jotted something. "Here's the telephone number of this cottage. Call us if anyone strange comes to town."

"Define strange."

"Scary-looking guys."

"Like you?"

Ciara smiled and Griff eyed her.

"Yeah, like me, only bigger, meaner looking. There's another fifty bucks for you if you see someone and call us, but don't come out here. If I see you again on this property, you're out the money and I'll let your dad know you've been using this place for parties, got it?"

"Yeah." Snatching the fifty, he ambled to the front door and hesitated. "Are you guys hiding from the cops?"

"No, we're just looking for peace and quiet."

"There's tons of that out here. It's quiet and boring."

The kid left and Ciara went to the window. His friends got back into the truck and they took off.

"You think he'll report us to his dad?"

"Why don't you call the dad first and we'll avoid any confusion."

She made the call and explained the situation, that she'd inherited the cottage and this was the first chance she had to visit. Luckily the property hadn't been booked so he said they could stay for a week if they wanted.

A week alone with Griff? Under different circumstances she might have welcomed the offer. But right now they needed to focus on staying alive.

She hung up. "Everything's good."

From behind her, Griff placed his hand on her shoulder. She closed her eyes, appreciating the comfort of his touch.

"What I wouldn't give for a few hours without an adrenaline rush," she said.

"Why don't you take a bath and relax? I'll keep watch."

"Thanks." She started for the bathroom and hesitated. "Could you do me a favor?"

"What's that?"

"Teach me how to defend myself?"

"You seem to be doing pretty good with hairspray and blenders."

"Please?"

"I told you, as long as I'm around—"

"No offense, but in your line of work I'm guessing you won't be around forever, and you definitely won't be in my life forever, so just a few moves or something?"

"If it will make you feel better."

"It will. I'm tired of being scared and helpless all the time."

She opened the bathroom door. "I know this is just another job for you, but I wanted to say thanks, for protecting me."

"Sure."

Ciara went into the bathroom, drew the bath and then pressed her back against the door. She'd never relied on anyone before. Even when Gran was alive Ciara was the strong one, brainstorming strategies to increase business. She was a take-charge person in every way except physically considering her five-foot-three-inch height and one hundred and fifteen pounds. But then, as a preschool teacher–turned museum owner, who would have thought she'd need to learn self-defense?

Who would have thought she'd be hiding out on Whidbey Island with a dangerous and handsome spy? That's what he was, right, a spy, even though he didn't call himself that?

She found a welcome basket of bath products including bubbles and shampoo. The goons may still be after them, but she was going to pretend for thirty minutes that they were safe so her blood pressure could get back to normal.

Uh, right. Normal. With Griffin Black in the next room.

She couldn't help being drawn to the complicated man who seemed violent in some ways and tender in others. He was an enigma, another good reason to keep her emotional distance. Heck, she'd thought Thom was a nice, polite man and he turned out to be a lying bastard. She knew Griff lived a life of deceit and violence. She wouldn't be stupid enough to fall for him, even if his motives were honorable since he was trying to save lives.

Griffin Black was a ghost, a man who'd probably kissed hundreds of women in the line of duty, a man who'd take your heart along with your secrets when he disappeared into the mist.

"I'm just tired," she whispered to herself.

And still scared. She knew Griff would abandon her once he found the microchips and completed his assignment. She'd be abandoned and her life would lay shredded at her feet. Would the terrorists ever stop looking for her?

Shaking off rising panic, she shucked her clothes and got into the warm water. Sinking down, she closed her eyes, and pictured better, sweeter times in her mind. She remembered visiting the Queen Mary Tea Room with Gran, taking the Clipper up to Victoria and spending a long weekend in the Cascade Mountains. With those tender memories came the fear that she'd never get to experience that kind of peace again.

She started to drift, like she had in the car. What was the matter with her? Lack of food, probably. The clam chowder was tasty, but she couldn't bring herself to eat much because her stomach had been in knots over her situation.

Gran a smuggler? She was a sweet, generous woman

who struggled with her own finances because she gave so much away. She was not a criminal and she would surely not be a party to smuggling weapons that could kill people.

Griff knocked softly on the door.

"Yes?" She sat up. That's when she realized she hadn't locked the door. Her pulse raced against her throat. Talk about feeling extremely vulnerable.

"I'm making coffee. How do you take yours?"

"Is there any tea?"

"I'll look."

She stepped out of the tub and dried off, grateful for the terry-cloth guest robe hanging on the door. She welcomed being out of her restrictive clothing. The elastic of her pants was cutting into her sides, and the slip-on shoes Griff bought her were too tight in the toes. She didn't want to point out the fact that she had duck feet.

Not that he'd care. He thought of her as his assignment, not as a woman. She washed her face and found lotion in the basket of goodies. Feeling almost normal, she took a deep breath. *You can't avoid him forever.*

But she wanted to. Being around Griff was a constant reminder of how her life had gone from normal to chaotic. She couldn't change her situation, but she could deal with it head-on.

"Get a backbone, girl," she said to her reflection.

GRIFF hesitated before going back to the kitchen to make her tea. She'd been in there for half an hour. Women didn't spend that much time in the bathtub, did they? How would he know? The only woman he'd gotten remotely close to was Mary, and they'd never lived together.

He pushed back his usual guilt of having involved someone in his dangerous line of work. Ciara was in danger, sure, but not because of him. He had no reason to feel guilty about her situation.

He'd feel less guilty if he dropped her off where she'd be out of the way and safe.

He filled a pot with water and turned on the stove, then pulled out his phone and called Dalton Keen.

"Keen."

"Griffin Black."

"What, did I send you the wrong brand of whiskey?"

"You got the brand right, but it was totally unnecessary. I was only doing my job."

"And mine, as well. To what do I owe the honor?"

"I need your help on my current assignment. I'm tracking down microchips before they end up in enemy hands and installed in jet engines on Monday."

"Terrorists attempting complete access to a plane. Got it. What can I do?"

"How big is your place?"

"Big enough for the local handyman."

"Interesting choice of cover."

"Wasn't mine. My objective is to stay under the radar and recuperate. What's your cover?"

"Doesn't matter. It's been blown. I have to drop something off with you for safe-keeping."

"Something?" Keen asked.

"A woman."

"A witness?"

"Originally she was a suspect, but that's no longer the case."

"She single?"

"Excuse me?"

"Sorry, forgot you have no sense of humor."

Griff used to have one. "We're on the run from the terrorists who want the chips. I think we lost them back in Seattle, but these bastards are relentless. They've been able to track us like a shadow."

"And you're positive the woman isn't hitting for the other team?"

He hesitated. "Yes."

"How can I help?"

"Be there and be charming when we arrive tomorrow, probably late. I have a feeling she's not going to like this plan."

"She's taken to her rescuer?"

"It'll pass."

"You hope. You need anything else besides hiding your girl?"

His chest swelled. For a second he liked the feeling that Ciara was *his* girl, this sweet, kind creature who somehow polished his sharp edges into something smooth and likable.

Fool.

"Why, you looking for something to keep you occupied?" Griff asked.

"I'm losing my flippin' mind out here."

Griff felt for the guy. He was used to being in the field, rescuing hostages, not being stuck in a small town in a remote corner of the country.

"You good with IT stuff?" Griff said.

"I'm no techno geek, but I do okay."

"I need to access to delivery logs for anything coming into the local ports. See if you can track the name Ruth O'Malley, or—" He paused. "Ciara O'Malley."

Who knows, they could be using her name, even if

she wasn't playing for their team. As a matter of fact, he wondered if whoever was behind this conspiracy was using the O'Malley name in hopes of setting up Ciara to take the fall if plans went south.

"I'll give you a call when I find something," Dalton said.

"Great, and Keen?"

"Yeah?"

"I owe you. For taking her off my hands."

"Man, I owe you for my life, remember? I'll see you tomorrow."

Griff ended the call and turned to pour hot water. There stood Ciara, in a white robe, her cheeks flushed. Great, how much had she heard?

"I found something," she said. She crooked her finger and he followed her into the bedroom. "There's a linen closet in here," she explained, as if making clear she had no reason to lure him into the bedroom other than business.

Of course, he knew that.

"I was looking for an extra towel to dry my hair and found this locked closet." She crossed her arms over her chest and looked at him, waiting. "It might be a storage closet."

"Might be." He pulled a pick from his wallet and realized he'd been so focused on staying alive that he hadn't gone in search of the smuggled dolls. He and Ciara were in constant and serious danger, never knowing from where the next assault would come.

And he didn't want to see Ciara hurt. Not good. Tomorrow couldn't come soon enough. With her hidden at Keen's place, Griff could fully focus on his job.

The lock clicked and he swung open the door. Sure enough there were half a dozen packages—shipped from all over the world, stacked neatly inside—along with a lock box.

"How did you know they'd be here?" he said, once again questioning if her charm had blinded him to the fact that she was involved in this conspiracy.

"You are such a jerk," she said, reading his thoughts. "I'll bet we'll find answers in here." She grabbed the lock box and headed into the front room.

He grabbed a few packages and followed, placing them on the kitchen counter. He turned to find her aiming a butcher knife at him.

"For the boxes," she said, with a smirk.

He suspected she was tempted to use it on him at the moment. It was natural for him to suspect everyone, all the time.

"Can you pick the lock on that?" She nodded toward the gray lock box.

"Yep." In minutes he'd opened the personal safe. Photographs and a bankbook. They could wait.

He moved the dining room place settings aside and went to work on the packages, cutting through the seams of the first box.

Her cell phone chimed a silly tune and she dug into her purse.

"Don't answer it," he said.

She eyed the phone. "It's Adele. She's running my business, I have to."

"Don't tell her where you are."

She turned her back to him and took the call.

"Hey, Adele. How's it going? Oh, good, I'm glad…. Uh-huh. Yes…sure."

Ciara leaned against the kitchen counter and rubbed her neck. He guessed the older woman chattered on because Ciara had that look on her face that his mom got when Aunt Sandra used to call.

Griff went back to his package, opening the flaps to reveal an American Girl doll. Bingo, these had to be the dolls carrying the microchips. But when he scanned the eyes with the D.R., it read negative. He analyzed a second doll, which read nothing at first, but on the second pass over its green, glass eye, the reader flared orange. He put that doll aside and went to the bedroom to pull out the remaining boxes.

"Yes, it's wonderful," Ciara said to her caller as he passed. "Romantic doesn't even begin to describe it." She rolled her eyes, but was doing a good sell job to her friend.

He started on the last packages.

"Probably Monday, I'm not sure yet. How does that work with your schedule? I can call Jenny for backup if you have plans. Okay, great. Sure, but…"

Phone to her ear she collapsed on the sofa and swung her legs over the arm. Out of the corner of his eye he spotted bare legs all the way up to her thighs.

Focus.

He pulled out another American Girl doll and scanned her eyes. Another orange flare-up. A sense of relief washed over him. He had two out of three. This assignment might come to a close sooner than he thought.

When he analyzed the last three dolls he came up empty. There was still one chip out there. And he had seventy-two hours to find it.

He glanced at Ciara, who looked dangerously close to falling asleep. He took the phone from her hand.

"Adele, it's Griffin Black."

"Oh, Mr. Black, I can't thank you enough for taking Ciara to the islands for some rest and recreation."

The islands? Did Ciara tell the old woman where they were after he'd specifically asked her not to?

"Ciara's really wiped out from all the driving today, so how about I have her call you back tomorrow?"

"That would be wonderful. And would you mind bringing back some fresh fruit and vegetables from the organic farms out there?"

"I'll see what I can do. Good night." He clicked the Off button. "I told you not to tell her where we were."

"I didn't," she said. "The Feds told her we were spotted heading north. I guess she just assumed we'd do the romantic thing in the San Juans or something."

"The Feds?"

"Yeah, she said they were looking for me before when I called her from your car, but—"

"And you didn't tell me?" He towered over her.

"You were too busy yelling at me for calling her, and then avoiding arrest for abusing your girlfriend, remember?"

"What did she say about the Feds?"

"That two agents stopped by asking about me. That's it. I turned off the phone on the drive up here to conserve battery and when I turned it back on she called immediately."

"She's nosy."

"She cares. I realize that's hard for you to understand, but people do care about each other."

He fought back memories of his older sister mothering him when they were kids. He'd hated it at the time, but desperately hated it being stolen from him as an adult.

"What's the verdict on the boxes of dolls?" she said.

"I may have found two chips."

"Two? How many are there?"

"Three. There's one more out there."

He raised one of the two chip-positive dolls above his head to smash it open against the counter.

"Hey!" she protested.

He hesitated.

"Gentle." Shaking her head, she went to the dining-room table and sat down. Grabbing the doll, she said, "Sometimes you can get inside without having to destroy it. Let me take a look."

She brushed her fingertips across the doll's cheeks as if it were a breathing, flesh-and-blood child, then up to her hairline. His body was reacting in ways it shouldn't. The lack of sleep the last few days was messing with his head.

"With these particular dolls you can sometimes pop the head right off." With a snap, she removed the head and handed it to him. "See? No damage."

He ran the card reader over the doll's left eye, then her right. It flared the location in the right eye. He pointed his knife at the corner of the glass eyeball.

"Do you have to dig her eye out?"

He looked at her. "I can do this in the other room if you want."

"What about sticking your finger in there first. Maybe it's not in the glass itself, but it's behind the back of the eyeball."

He shook his head.

"It's worth a try."

Griff ran his fingers inside the doll's head and felt nothing unusual. "Sorry, I'm going to have to do surgery."

She picked up another doll and analyzed it, probably because she couldn't bear to watch what he was going to do next.

"This one, too?" she asked.

"No, that one's clean."

She stroked its hair. He snapped his attention back to the procedure, and as gently as possible dug out the glass eye, creating a haunted expression on the doll's face. He placed it on the dining table and went into the kitchen in search of something solid and heavy to smash the eyeball.

She came up beside him, snatched a dishtowel and searched the drawers. She grabbed tape from a kitchen drawer and went back to the table. He told himself he didn't care what she was doing, yet his body was hyper-aware of her every move.

He found a meat mallet, placed the eyeball on a bed of paper towels and smashed the glass. Amidst the shards he found a small computer chip, a quarter of an inch in diameter. With the tip of a steak knife he brushed the chip clear of debris and pulled a small glass tube from his pocket. He deposited the chip safely in the tube.

"You're not going to destroy it?" she said, studying him.

"We need to keep at least one intact so researchers can figure out a way to neutralize the program in this chip if it accidentally ends up in a jet engine."

Ciara shuddered at the thought of what the micro-chips could do, the deaths they could cause. How could anyone be involved in such devastation?

She focused on the contents of the lockbox, hoping to find something to ease the anxiety brewing in her stomach. Pulling out a stack of photos, she smiled at the top picture of her and Gran on the ferry to Victoria.

"I guess this really is Gran's place," she said, paging through the photos. Sadness filled her chest. Gran was the one family member who'd nurtured Ciara, loved her unconditionally.

Her eyes caught on a dark-blue checkbook. She opened it and gasped at the balance: fifty-seven thousand dollars.

Ciara pushed back from the table and stood.

"Ciara?" Griff questioned.

"There's thousands in there," she said, unable to tear her eyes from the bankbook. "Where would she get that kind of money? Oh, no."

Disgust filled her chest. Expenses at the museum were sometimes covered by the reserve account, supposedly created from Gran's retirement, when their monthly income didn't support the business.

"Have I been using this, this blood money? My God, she made me into a criminal. Why, Griff?" She struggled to focus on him through the tears in her eyes. "How could she do this to me?"

An ACHE of betrayal pierced Griff's chest as Ciara struggled to make sense of her world. A world that had just burned to ash at her feet.

"I'm sorry," he said, stepping toward her. He wanted to wipe that distraught look from her eyes.

Hell, he *had* gone soft. He should be worried about finding the third microchip, not offering her a comforting shoulder to cry on.

"Everything she gave me, the collectible dolls, the armoire, my necklace." She grabbed the charm at her throat and ripped it off. "She gave this to me after my breakup with Thom so I wouldn't shut myself off from people. She said that just like Tinkerbell needs people to believe in her to live, we need people, too."

She hurled the necklace across the room and raced into the bedroom, slamming the door.

Now what? He didn't know how to counsel a woman whose world had been shattered. He wasn't the counseling type.

Focus on the mission, he told himself.

Analyzing the deposits and withdrawals in the bankbook, he spotted quite a few checks made out to WIT. An accomplice, perhaps?

Griff went back to dissecting the second doll, removing the chip and placing it in the tube. That's when he noticed the eye patch on the first doll. Ciara's handiwork.

He glanced at the bedroom door, regretting that he couldn't do more to help her somehow.

It's not your job to help her. Yet she was an innocent, like his sister, Beth. Ciara had been betrayed not by strangers, but by someone she trusted, someone who loved her.

He picked up her fairy necklace and slipped it into his pocket. He cursed Ciara's grandmother for putting Ciara's life in danger, for lying to such a trusting, sweet person.

Griff knocked on the bedroom door. "Ciara?"

The door swung open and she stormed out, fully dressed. "What do we do next?"

She went into the main room and turned to him, her eyes filled with anger.

"Do you need to talk?" he said.

"No, I need to scream, cry and hit something."

He reached out, but she stepped away. "Everything I have, everything I believed in, it's all gone." She paced the living room. "My salary, the dolls, my car." She turned to him. "Gran helped me buy that car. What about my salary since I took over? Is it…is it all blood money?"

"I don't know."

To think she'd been so innocent and untouched by the

ugliness of his world until a few minutes ago. He wanted to teleport her back there, back to that place of blissful ignorance where life seemed so simple.

The phone rang, and the hair bristled at the back of his neck.

"Get down!" He threw her to the ground just as a bullet crashed through the window.

Chapter Eight

Ciara gasped for air, pinned to the hardwood floor by Griff. "Get off me!"

"Be still, damn it. Someone's shooting at us."

They waited, his breath warming the back of her neck.

"Come," he ordered, slipping off her. They took cover in the kitchen.

As he reached up and grabbed his gun from the counter, a shot cracked the oven glass. She shrieked, and her body trembled uncontrollably.

He pulled her against his chest. "Shh. You're going to be okay. I promise."

"You're full…of it," she stuttered in fear.

"I need you to be fearless and take orders. Can you do that?"

She nodded, hating the sound of her frightened voice.

He edged his way up the wall and spied out the window. "I see one car. I'll draw fire, and you get to my car, got it?"

"But—"

"Be a good soldier and don't question me." He placed his keys in her hand. "It's how we'll stay alive."

She nodded, appreciating the strength in his blue

eyes. Her life had been blasted apart, and the only thing she had left was this man, this violent stranger.

Who'd just promised her she'd be okay.

Taking her hand, he led her to the living area. She snatched her purse from the floor as they crawled to the side door.

"From the angle of the shot, I figure he's out back with a clear view of the living room," he said. "When you hear me fire, get to the car and wait for me. Stay low so he can't see you."

She nodded, her pulse pounding in her ears.

And then he kissed her, a brief touch of their lips that sent a shiver across her shoulders.

"Good luck," he said.

It felt like good-*bye* and she wanted to protest, but knew her best chance of staying alive was to do what he said.

With a nod he swung the front door open. Bullets pelleted a kitchen chair, a vase and a lamp across the room.

Griff sprung to his feet and started firing. "Go!" he ordered.

She raced to the car, climbing inside and curling up in the front seat, clutching her purse. She shoved the key in the ignition to be ready to go when Griff showed up.

Gunshots echoed off the water and she squeezed her eyes shut. They had to be from Griff's gun because their attacker was using a silencer. She hoped Griff nailed the bastard and then prayed that Griff wouldn't be shot.

What felt like fifteen minutes passed. Nothing. No Griff, no more gunshots. She steadied her breath, trying to plan what to do next if Griff didn't show. She wouldn't fall apart. But her insides started to unravel at the thought of Griff being killed.

Something slammed against the driver's window and she screamed, then caught sight of Griff's pained expression. She unlocked the door and he ripped it open, then fell to his knees.

"Glove box, my other weapon," he said, breathing heavy.

She grabbed the gun from the glove box and handed it to him.

"You need to get the hell out of here," he ordered.

"No, I won't—"

"Listen to me. Get the chips to Dalton Keen. You have his contact information." He placed the small glass tube with the microchips in her hand.

That's when she noticed his hand was smeared with blood.

"Griff, you've been shot? I can't leave you."

With a deep breath he pushed away. "Damn it, Ciara, make my death count for something."

His death? A chill settled across her shoulders. No, he couldn't mean…

"Go!" he shouted.

Terrified, she shoved the car in gear and took off. In the rearview mirror she spotted Griff tackle the shooter as he tried to get into his car to chase after her.

Griff was buying Ciara time, time to save her life and get the microchips to the right people.

Make my death count for something.

This wasn't right. The ground had been ripped out from under her when she'd discovered Gran was a smuggler. Nothing was real anymore; nothing made sense.

Nothing but Griff's integrity and honor. He could have dumped her, left her behind to be tortured by terrorists. But he didn't. He risked his life over and over again to protect her.

And he was going to die to protect a weak, naïve woman, the granddaughter of a criminal.

Anger ripped through her body at the thought of an honorable man dying because of something her grandmother did.

She spun the car around and flashed her bright lights at the house. A tall, broad-shouldered man repeatedly kicked Griff in the stomach then he pulled out his gun. Griff was going to die.

"No!" she cried, honking the horn. She floored it and ducked as two bullets bounced off the windshield of Griff's car. It was then she realized he had bulletproof glass.

Squeezing the steering wheel she clenched her teeth and aimed for the bastard. She'd never killed a man before, heck, she shooed spiders out of her apartment rather than squash them.

But she was no longer that sweet, innocent girl. The shooter got a few more shots off and realizing it was pointless, turned and raced toward the cliffs in the distance. At least she'd distracted him from shooting Griff at point-blank range. She shoved her foot down on the accelerator, closing in on the guy, wanting him dead, wanting all of them out of her life.

The shooter glanced over his shoulder, saw her closing in and jumped.

And just like that, he was gone. She slammed on the breaks and spun the wheel to the left, the car stopping dangerously close to the edge. Adrenaline pumped through her body. If he'd found her it was a matter of time before the rest of them did. She had to get Griff into the car and get out of here.

Gripping the steering wheel, she fought back a sob building in her chest. She'd just chased a man over a cliff to his death. She no longer knew who she was.

But she knew she wanted to live.

She pulled up to Griff's lifeless body and got out of the car. Kneeling beside him, she brushed hair from his forehead. "Griff? Can you hear me?"

He moaned and blinked a few times before fully opening his eyes. He grabbed her wrist and squeezed. "What are you doing here? The shooter...where?" He strained to see beyond her.

"He's gone. I took care of him."

"You? I told you to get the hell out of here."

"I'm a bad soldier, I know. Now sit up so I can get you into the car."

"You have the chips," he said, as he collapsed in the passenger seat. "I told you to find Keen. I ordered you—"

She slammed the door on his protest.

"Thanks for coming back for me, Ciara. Thanks for killing a guy to save my life," she muttered.

She got behind wheel and shoved the car in Drive, ignoring his rant.

"You defied me. If they would have gotten those chips...the planes..." He closed his eyes and she thought he might have passed out. Then he whispered, "Beth."

"Who's Beth?"

He shook his head, indicating he was conscious and the subject was off-limits. Gripping his shoulder, he winced and leaned back against the seat.

"What is it? You've been shot?" She slowed down.

"Don't stop. Keep going. Need to get out of here, get to Dalton Keen."

"We need to get you to a hospital."

"No, they'll find us, easy to find us if I'm brought in. They have to report gunshot victim to cops. Questions. Paperwork. Will slow me down."

"Can I pick you up anything? Antibiotic ointment, gauze, anything?"

"Just drive." He hunched lower in the seat and his head tipped to the side. This time he did pass out.

Looks like you're on your own, Ciara.

Reality shook her to the core. She'd gone from being a former preschool teacher to saving a government agent's life. Not just any agent, but Griff, a man she felt oddly connected to.

"A bit twisted, Ciara," she whispered, thinking about how he'd drugged her, kidnapped her and restrained her.

Yet now she understood. She was unwittingly involved in the smuggling business and he was determined to save innocents from the insanity of terrorism.

She wished she could seek medical help, but he was right; they didn't want to draw attention to themselves.

Okay, what next? She'd find a grocery or drugstore, buy supplies and tend his wound. Remembering the ABCs of first aid she'd learned as a teacher, she mentally checked off what she'd need: alcohol, gauze, tape. Maybe even two kinds of alcohol, one to use on his wound and the other for him to drink to dull the pain.

She remembered him drinking whiskey at his apartment. Depending on how serious his injury was, he might need it. But they only sold the hard stuff at state liquor stores in Washington and those closed by seven. Wine would have to do.

Once she got to the next town she'd assess his injury and make her list. It probably wouldn't hurt to contact

Dalton Keen and let him know what was happening, that they'd been found again, and so easily.

The memory of Griff asking her to undress in the woods filled her thoughts. He knew she'd been tagged with a tracking device but she'd left both the device and her clothes behind. How was it possible that they'd been tracked with such ease?

And who sent the shooter? Did he belong to the same group as the husky guy and dirty cop?

"One question at a time," she said aloud. "How did they find you?"

Did the terrorists have cells located on this lovely island getaway? The shooter found her and Griff too quickly, as if he was waiting for them. Or were she and Griff still being tracked?

She had to assume Griff was clean because he was a professional, which meant Ciara was being tracked somehow. If she didn't figure out how, she could flee to the Antarctic and they'd still find her.

She pulled off the road, grabbed her purse and got out. Emptying the contents on the hood of the car, she used her keychain penlight to analyze each and every item: notebook, wallet, keys, emery board. Nothing seemed unusual. She eyed her cell phone.

"Of course." Were they tracing her calls? Or were they tracking her through a GPS chip in the phone itself? Couldn't risk it. She tossed the phone into Puget Sound.

She was starting to think like a secret agent.

"Ciara!" Griff called, opening his door.

She ran to his side and encouraged him to stay in the car. "It's okay, I'm fine, everything's fine."

"Where did you go?" he said, panic in his eyes.

Her heart warmed. He cared about her.

"The microchips," he whispered.

So much for sentiment. "Here." She placed the tube in his hand and closed his fingers. "You hold on to it."

"Why did you get out of the car?"

"I was trying to figure out how they found us. I got rid of my cell phone."

He squinted as if trying to understand her actions.

"Either they traced Adele's call from the museum, or they're tracking me through the GPS. Sit back. We've got to keep moving."

He touched her arm, gently this time. "You're smart and cute."

Oh, boy, he must be hallucinating. "Yeah, thanks."

She grabbed her purse and got into the car. "I'm going to stop at a grocery store, get supplies and patch you up," she said to a semiconscious Griff.

He clenched his jaw, probably against the pain of his gunshot wound. She couldn't help but wonder why he chose this line of work.

She'd ask him later, after she stabilized his condition. Who did she think she was? Sure she'd fixed boo-boos for the kids at the preschool, but clean and bandage a gunshot wound?

You can do anything if you put your mind to it.

Words from Gran, the woman who had been Ciara's champion, a woman who in reality was a traitor to her country.

What Ciara wouldn't give for answers, answers to why Gran had lied to her all these years, why she'd betrayed her country and broken the law. It just didn't make sense.

It's not like she had expensive tastes. Gran always

struggled to make her bills, yet she had thousands of dollars sitting in a bank account?

"Why, Gran?" Ciara whispered. "Why?"

GRIFF was being tortured with a cattle prod, burning his shoulder with a searing, hot iron. "No," he swung at his tormentor.

"Stop!" a female ordered.

A familiar female voice. Beth? Maybe he wasn't being tortured. Maybe his big sister was patching him after a fall from the weeping willow out back.

"Beth," he said.

"Beth's not here."

Then it all rushed back: the phone call, the helplessness, the devastation.

She was gone. A victim of mindless, mass destruction.

"You need to let me do this," the female said.

If not Beth, then who? An enemy agent assigned to torture information out of him? No, he'd never allow himself to be caught and imprisoned by his enemy. He'd die first.

"Who, where am I?" He struggled to open his eyes.

"Shh, it's okay," she said.

Beth was now an angel watching over him. Even in death she cared for him.

"I need to finish dressing the wound. Can you keep still? Do you want some more wine?"

Figures his sister would offer the weak stuff. She didn't like his propensity for whiskey, his best friend on days he couldn't stop thinking about Beth's last minutes of life.

A bottle was held to his lips and he swallowed, then opened his eyes and was staring into emerald-green eyes.

"Where's Beth?"

"I don't know. I'm Ciara, remember?"

Ciara. He mentally thrashed through the last few days, those eyes, striking, hypnotic. Something about those remarkable eyes...

A weapon was hiding inside her green eyes. No, not her eyes, but a doll's eyes.

"The doll lady?" he said.

"That's me. Now keep still so I can dress the wound."

"What happened?"

"You were shot in the shoulder. It's okay. I'm fixing it."

"You promised you'd leave, take the chips."

"Nope, never promised."

Her expression tightened as she did something to his shoulder. He closed his eyes against the searing pain and used his breathing to focus through it, letting the pain flow through him and out, a technique he'd learned in AW-21 training.

"Good, that's it. Okay, now take some of these."

He blinked and opened his eyes. She offered small white pills pinched between her fingers.

"What are they?"

"Pain reliever."

She placed them in his mouth and picked up the bottle of wine.

"Water?" he said.

"Sure." She cracked open a plastic bottle and held it to his lips. "Sit up a little, that's it."

She opened her mouth slightly as if mimicking his drinking of the water. He swallowed and leaned back against the seat. She cleaned up the first aid supplies, stuffing bloody rags into a garbage bag and tying it. He reached up and felt his shoulder. She'd bandaged him pretty well for an amateur.

"You shouldn't have come back for me," he said.

She tossed the garbage bag of bloody towels into the back seat. "I'm done having this conversation. We need to get to the ferry."

"Doesn't leave until the morning."

"There's one at eleven."

"Need reservations."

"It's worth a shot," she said, wincing at her choice of words. "Sorry. Duh." Shaking her head, she pulled out of the parking lot.

"How did you know how to do this?" He motioned to his shoulder.

"I was a preschool teacher."

"Yeah? I didn't know preschoolers needed triage."

"We had to learn basic first aid. Now I'm glad I did," she said, eyeing his wound. "What do we do next, other than find you a real doctor?"

"Figure out the identity of the smuggler."

"I thought we covered that already. It's Gran." Her voice cracked.

Griff looked away, not wanting to feel too much of her pain for fear he'd completely lose his focus. It was bad enough that he had to accept the fact she'd come back for him. He'd told her to run, to find safety in the protection of Dalton Keen. Instead, she'd risked her life to save him. She cared about him. And it felt good.

Don't be a fool.

"Your grandmother's been gone for six months, but there could be someone else on the inside."

"It could be me," she offered.

He glanced at her and forced a smile. "No, it couldn't."

Gratitude filled her green eyes. He could tell she

needed someone to believe in her. The guilt must be tearing her apart.

"I'm thinking it's someone who works for you or maybe one of your volunteers?"

"Let's see, Lucinda flies around the world, visiting all kinds of interesting places: Korea, Laos, Moscow. It wouldn't surprise me if she was into something illegal."

"Who else, anyone who might have access to your computer at work?"

"Adele, you've met her." She shook her head as if the thought was ridiculous. "Pete Desai, our computer guy. As a matter of fact, he recently stopped accepting payment for his computer services."

"Really?"

"Yep. He wants me to take him to lunch instead."

"He's got a crush on you?"

"I doubt that."

"I don't. Can you think of anyone else?"

"There's my accountant, Dean. He's got the pass-codes so he can do our payroll and taxes."

"I'll make a call when we get to Dalton's place and do some more background checks, see if anything pops. And we'll find out what he's uncovered. That's it, just those four?"

"A few high school girls, Jenny and Amelia, come in on weekends to help with parties, but they don't do much in the office itself. I don't know. None of these people seem like..." Her voice trailed off.

"What?"

"I was going to say none of them seem like terrorists. Stupid thing to say considering Gran was one."

"The chip smuggling is a recent thing. We don't know your grandmother was involved."

"But she was a smuggler."

He didn't answer. A few minutes of silence passed.

"We're not necessarily looking for a terrorist," he said. "We're looking for a mercenary, someone who loves money more than his or her own integrity."

"If you check on Pete's background and he's okay, how about I call him and have him set up remote access? Then we can go through museum computer files and look for something suspicious, or a trail or something."

"Okay, agent fifty-five," he joked, trying to cover that he felt woozy. Was it from the wine or blood loss? Whatever the case, he needed to stay conscious. "I'm sorry about all this," he said, not sure what else to talk about. They had nothing in common other than this mission.

"Yeah, well, I'm too damn naive for my own good."

"Come again?"

"Someone was smuggling weapons through my museum and I didn't even have an inkling. How stupid am I?"

"These people are professionals. Who knows, maybe the smuggler doesn't know he or she is doing it. Maybe they think they're ordering collectible dolls for a customer."

"Nice try, but from the look of Gran's bank account it's obvious she knew what she was doing. No dolls are worth that kind of money."

"The balance was higher a few months before her death," he said.

"How much higher?"

"A few hundred thousand dollars' worth."

She shook her head.

"Your grandmother made out checks to something called WIT. Ring any bells?"

"Nope, sorry. I came on a few months after her death. Adele offered to run the place, but I couldn't do that to her. The woman has a family and grandchildren. I didn't want to saddle her with the museum."

"So you took it over for your grandmother, giving up your teaching career?"

"I felt I owed it to Gran. It's the family business, the only real ties I have to family. Had to family, a criminal family. What a loser."

"You shouldn't define yourself by your family's mistakes."

"Kind of hard not to."

He glanced outside into the darkness, fighting back his own sense of failure. He couldn't help but go there. This assignment was supposed to be a simple case of finding one microchip in one doll and bringing it back for analysis.

When had a mission, or life for that matter, ever been simple? Especially this one, involving a sweet, determined woman like Ciara who trusted and believed in her grandmother, only to have that trust destroyed by the truth?

He must have drifted again, because when he opened his eyes, the car was next to the ferry pay booth.

"I know we don't have a reservation, but we're desperate to get home," Ciara said in a tired voice. "My husband's had a fever for two days and we were stranded in the pass and slept in the car and had no decent food and there was no reception so we couldn't make a reservation. Are you sure there isn't room for one more car on the ferry tonight?"

The guy in the booth sighed. "Okay, fine. Fourteen fifty."

"Thank you, thank you so much."

Griff started to reach for his wallet.

"Don't," she said, nodding at his jacket that gapped in front.

Good point, if the guy got a look at Griff's bloody shirt, they'd be going to jail, not to Port Townsend.

She paid the fare and pulled onto the ferry. Griff wouldn't relax until the boat left, headed for backup in the form of Dalton Keen.

She cracked both their windows and turned the radio to a swing music station. A few minutes later the boat started across the water.

"I need some air," she said.

"But—"

"I'll be right there." She pointed to the railing beside the car. "Not far."

She got out and leaned against the railing, letting the wind blow her hair away from her face. When she closed her eyes and tipped her chin, he marveled at how she looked like a goddess, a warrior goddess.

Who'd saved his life.

He didn't like being obligated to anyone, especially civilians, and especially a civilian he knew he'd have to leave behind.

He couldn't look away, mesmerized by the moonlight casting a warm glow on her cheeks and illuminating flecks of gold in her red hair.

Suddenly she turned to him and he read panic in her eyes. "Do you hear that?" she said through the open window.

"What?"

"The engines have stopped."

Chapter Nine

Biting back the pain, Griff opened his door and went to the railing. Sure enough, they were slowing down.

"Stay here." Griff crossed the lanes of parked cars and eyed the other side of the ferry. Nothing. No Coast Guard or other official law enforcement boat had come up beside them. This could be a mere traffic issue, but this late at night?

He went back to Ciara. "Put the bag of towels and anything with my blood on it in the trunk," he ordered, gripping his shoulder. "Grab my overnight bag and we'll head up to the top deck."

"What's the plan?"

"It doesn't look like we're being boarded. But they might have called in our description to ferry officials. We should abandon the car and find someplace to hide. It would help to change our appearances in case we're discovered."

"Yeah, like how am I going to change this?" She flipped her flaming-red hair.

"I've got something in my bag." He cupped her elbow and led her to the single-occupant bathroom on the car level. He locked the door and pulled out a bottle of black shoe polish. "Streak your hair with this."

She analyzed the bottle with a sad look.

"Streak a few strands and let them hang down around your face, then shove the rest into a baseball cap. I've got one in here somewhere." He dug into his bag and pulled out a Chicago White Sox cap.

"Lose the long-sleeve shirt, roll up your jeans to the knees. Here." He got a marker from the side pocket of his bag. "Draw a tattoo on your ankle, maybe on your upper arm. Get creative."

"Creative is my middle name," she muttered.

He cracked open the door and peered down the line of cars seeing nothing unusual or alarming. How could a terrorist agent influence ferry operation? Simple, someone could have called in and reported a terrorist threat in the form of Griff and Ciara driving a black BMW.

Sure, why not? The Washington State Department of Transportation had to take every threat seriously. Damn, would they ever get a break to recharge and strategize? This assignment had been one crisis after another.

It nearly ended back at the cottage. His attacker aimed his firearm and demanded Griff tell him where the redhead went.

Strange thing...the guy didn't even ask about the microchips. Why? Did they all assume she had them from the start?

Not good. That bull's-eye on her back was growing bigger by the minute.

He leaned over, unzipped his bag and grabbed a hat for himself, a Seattle Mariners hat, hoping if they had to leave the confines of the bathroom he would blend in. When he stood, he got the spins and took a slow, deep breath, pressing the back of his head to the wall.

"What is it?" Ciara placed her hand to his cheek.

He cracked open his eyes and remarked how different she looked with the black strands hanging down her cheeks, and her chest filling out the sleeveless shirt, exposing the soft, pale skin of her arms.

"Are you dizzy?" she whispered.

"I'm fine."

"Okay, macho man."

"Do you have anything to change into?"

"There's another shirt in there." He nodded toward the bag.

"Good. You're going to have to ditch the jacket, as well. Too bloody."

He shucked his jacket, then reached for his shirt buttons, but couldn't stop his fingers from trembling.

"I'm faster, move." She brushed his fingers away and in seconds, she'd unbuttoned his shirt and was slipping it off his shoulders.

She flushed at the sight of his naked chest and he wished they were two different people in a different circumstance.

"Get the hair gel," he said. "I'll slick it back to give me a different look."

"You've done this before?" she said.

"A few times."

She found the shirt and slipped it over his head. Her fingers felt so warm and gentle as she tugged it down over his torso.

"I got it," he said, wanting her to stop touching him like that. "Gel?"

She handed him the travel-size bottle and he squirted

some into his hand, but his eyes started to water and he couldn't focus.

"Women are better at this stuff than guys anyway." She scooped the gel from his hand and rubbed it between her palms, then finger-combed his hair.

He closed his eyes, enjoying her scalp massage a little too much.

"I'm going to pass out if you keep doing that," he said.

She stopped and rinsed her hands. "I'm sorry, was I hurting you?"

He caught her reflection in the mirror. "No, I'm exhausted and that felt really good."

She smiled and he had to remind himself why they were hiding in the bathroom. He glanced away and noticed the blood smearing his pants.

"Damn, if they find us I'm screwed with all this blood on my pants."

"Ah, but we have this, remember?" She dabbed at the bloodstains with the shoe polish and decorated the other side for balance.

"We're supposed to blend in when we leave the ferry," he protested.

"Yeah, like you've ever blended in with those eyes." She glanced up, embarrassed by her flirtatious comment. "How long do we have to stay in here?"

"Until the engines start up again."

"That could be…hours." She went white.

"What's wrong?"

"I need out," she said. "I can't stay in here."

Recognizing a panic attack, he opened the door, grabbed the bag and led her to the railing. "Shh, you're okay."

She gasped for breath.

"Focus on the lights in the distance," he said. "See them?" He rubbed her back.

"Yes."

"It will be okay." Yet her attack exposed them in a way he didn't need right now. He wanted to get back into hiding.

Suddenly the engines started up again.

"Is she okay?" a ferry worker asked.

"Just a little motion sickness."

"Helps if you go up top," he said.

"Why did the engines stop?" Griff asked, rubbing Ciara's back.

"Some idiot on a boat." He waved his hand. "The higher the better," he said to Ciara, whose hands clenched the railing.

"Thanks," Griff said.

He brushed his thumb against Ciara's cheek. "Did you hear that? We panicked for nothing. Still, I'm thinking we should walk off and leave the car in case they're waiting on the other end for us to drive off."

She nodded and focused on the shoreline.

"Want to try upstairs?"

"Sure."

He slung his bag over his shoulder and led her to the stairs. "You sit up front on the left where passengers get off, and I'll sit on the right."

"Why can't we sit together?"

"The less contact the better. Remember, they're looking for a couple traveling together. Between splitting up and your new hairstyle, well, that might throw them off for a little while, at least until we can reach help."

"Dalton Keen?"

"Yes."

They climbed the stairs to the passenger deck.

"Is he your partner or something?" she asked.

"I'm not the partner type. I did him a favor once and he's forever in my debt."

She eyed him in question.

"According to Keen," Griff clarified. "In this case, we could use his help."

"He's an agent, too?"

"On leave, but yes."

At the top of the stairs he hesitated and touched her shoulder. "You go ahead of me. I'll give you a minute so we don't look like we're together. Ready?"

She reached out and brushed the pad of her thumb across his cheek. "Yes. Be safe." With a wary smile she pushed through the door and disappeared.

Her resilience amazed him. Most victims or hostages fell apart when the gravity of their situation sunk in. But Ciara had turned her fear and anger into determination. She was an amazingly strong woman on the outside, but on the inside he knew she must be devastated and scared.

And he couldn't protect her if she was sitting across the ferry from him.

Not good, Black. His main objective had to be getting the microchips into the right hands—not protecting Ciara.

With a deep breath he left the stairwell and headed into the main passenger area. He didn't glance left, didn't look for her.

He tossed his bag to the floor between two vinyl seats and sat down, glancing at the window, hoping to see Ciara's reflection there.

When he didn't see anyone resembling her, he turned

and scanned the opposite side of the ferry. Nope, no White Sox cap, no sleeveless shirt. Panic clawed at his chest. Where the hell was she? He'd given her a good head start. She should be comfortably settled near the front of the ferry.

His eyes watered against the pain of his gunshot wound as he twisted and looked behind him. He was about to go in search of her when the door to the outside deck opened and Ciara breezed through holding her hat in place.

She glanced at him, only briefly, then flopped down on the seat. She must have needed the fresh air to fight off her anxiety.

He spied a Ciara-made tattoo on her upper arm, but couldn't quite make it out. He hadn't paid much attention before because he'd been more concerned with calming her panic attack. Wearing the muscle shirt and rolled up jeans and sporting a "tattoo," she looked like a biker's girlfriend, not a preschool teacher turned doll expert.

She was doing a good job of looking calm and relaxed, not stressed by the multiple threats on her life over the last twenty-four hours or the recent realization that her beloved grandmother was a criminal.

Ciara had a lot of guts for a woman, a kind of strength he didn't expect from her.

She glanced at him and he could have sworn he read thanks in her eyes. What for? He'd nearly abandoned her back at the cottage.

And he was about to abandon her with Dalton Keen.

Closing his eyes, he focused on slowing his pulse to recharge for a few minutes. He only had two, maybe three days to stop the final chip from getting into the wrong hands. He rubbed his thumb against the bump in his pocket. He was tempted to destroy the two chips, but if they didn't find the third, NSA experts would need the chip to figure out how to create one of their own to neutralize the technological weapon.

In all the insanity he hadn't notified Dalton they were on their way. He called him on his cell phone.

"Yeah?"

"Did I wake you?" Griff asked.

"If I slept."

Griff knew the feeling. The only place he found peace enough to sleep was at his retreat in Oregon that even his superiors didn't know about. Somehow he'd managed to keep that part of his life private.

"We're on our way," Griff said. "Should be there in twenty-five minutes."

"Sooner than I expected. What happened?"

"Doesn't matter. How's the search for mysterious packages going?"

"My skills weren't up to the job, but I had an expert look into it."

"Someone at base?"

"No, I called my baby brother. He's a primo computer geek. Broke into the FBI's mainframe once to prove a point."

"And he lived to tell about it?"

"He lived because he was a consultant for Locke Industries, the security giant, who'd been secretly hired by a task force to test the FBI system. Anyway, he's discovered two packages in transit ordered from the doll museum business account. One especially alarms me because it originated from the Middle East."

"They've been delivered?"

"Not yet. They're scheduled to hit the UPS Seattle warehouse early Saturday morning, just after midnight, then be delivered to Bellevue."

"And from Bellevue to the assembly for Monday's production. We need to red flag them as suspicious material."

"I'll handle it."

"Does it look to you like Ciara O'Malley is behind this?"

"Absolutely. She pays with a company credit card, knows the CID code, uses both her work account and her private e-mail, Tinkerbell4@gmail.com."

"Someone's getting into her e-mail accounts."

"Are you sure you're not getting any?"

"I wish."

"The truth comes out."

"She's an innocent, Keen."

"Yeah, when have I heard that before?" he joked.

"Are you going to help me or bust my chops?"

"I'll be at the ferry dock waiting for you."

"We're going to walk off and leave the car."

"I wouldn't. You'll draw attention to yourself."

"What would you suggest?"

"Follow me in your car and we'll find a safe spot to hide it."

"Ciara doesn't know I'm driving off. Can you find her and take her in your car? She's about five-foot-four, wearing a White Sox cap."

"Sure, when you get off the ferry, take a right into the first parking lot. It's a strip of stores. I'll get Ciara and meet you there."

"Good. Don't suppose you have any doctor friends in town? Someone you can trust?"

"I know a guy. Retired military."

"I should probably see him sooner than later."

"He's another night owl. I'll have him stop by tonight."

"Thanks. See you in a few minutes."

He glanced up and caught Ciara watching him. She smiled, and his heart beat a little faster. He wondered if Keen's doctor friend had a cure for that.

CIARA sensed Griff was uncomfortable when she looked at him, probably because they weren't supposed to know each other. Worried about his injury and his light-headedness, she couldn't help catching a glimpse now and then. She should be more worried about the bastard terrorist agents finding them.

It struck her like a fastball to the chest. She wouldn't be safe until Griff solved this case, and maybe not even then.

She shook off her trepidation. To stay alive she had to be tough and focus on helping Griff with this case. Then maybe she'd be safe.

When the ferry docked, she was one of the first passengers to get off. She ambled down the planks and eyed a park bench, but didn't want to expose herself under the shine of the street lamp.

She eyed the passenger walkway. No Griff. Now what? Cars started pulling off. What if he'd fallen asleep? Passed out from the gunshot wound? They'd find him and call an ambulance or police. Then she and Griff would be easy targets for the terrorists.

She started back toward the ferry.

"Ciara?" a man said.

She turned, fearing it was another terrorist assigned to track her down.

A tall, well-built man in his late twenties approached.

"I'm Dalton Keen. I was supposed to meet you when you got off the ferry."

"Oh." Her heart sank. Griff was passing her off to this agent.

"We're going to meet up with Griff at a strip mall around the corner," Dalton said.

She smiled with relief. He hadn't abandoned her after all.

Suddenly three police cars sped by and blocked the cars leaving the ferry terminal.

"This isn't good," Dalton said, placing his arm around her shoulder. "Come on."

"What about Griff?"

"Trust me. Pretend you're my girl, not Griff's." He winked.

He had such a trusting face, his left cheek dimpling when he smiled.

They walked to a nearby parking lot and he motioned for her to get inside his car. A pack of teenage boys pulled up to the curb and jumped out of an SUV. As they raced past to get a closer look at the excitement, Dalton called out, "What's going on?"

"There's a murderer on that ferry."

Chapter Ten

The kid tore off after his friends, who were restrained by ferry personnel.

Griff. They had to be referring to him, right? His enemies must have called in his description, hoping the local cops would mess things up by bringing him in. If Griff was in custody, then Ciara was on her own, exposed and easy prey.

"They did this to get to me?" she said.

"The microchips. You have them, right?"

"I gave them back to Griff."

"Not good."

"And he's been shot."

"Hell."

"I've got to help him." She stepped away from his car and Dalton placed his hand to her shoulder. Her eyes watered as she watched a dark-blue sedan being searched by the cops.

"You can't help him if you're in jail, too," Dalton said.

"Why can't he just identify himself as a federal officer?"

"Because technically he's nonexistent. It would just

confuse things. Besides, who knows if we can trust the local cops?"

"I could…"

"No, you couldn't. Griff is a resourceful soldier. If anyone can strategize his way out of this, it's Griff."

She eyed him. "You think so?"

"Yep, come on, get in the car. If they've got agents over here, chances are they're looking for you, too."

He opened her door and she slid inside. He joined her and turned on a scanner.

"How could they know we were headed to Port Townsend?" she said.

He put his index finger to his lips and pointed to the scanner. The guy looked so young to be an agent for the government, young, yet cynical, beaten down by life.

"Someone reported shots fired in Langley," a voice said over the scanner. "Description sounds like the same suspect who discharged his weapon at a storage unit in Everett. Six-two, dark hair, blue eyes, leather jacket, driving a black BMW. A woman is traveling with him. We think she might be a hostage."

"Me? They think I'm a hostage?"

"He's screwed," Dalton said, dialing his cell. "Come on, Griff, answer."

"He was going to walk off and leave the car," she explained.

"I talked him out of it. An abandoned car would draw too much attention. We were going to ditch the car, but he had no way of telling you that, so he sent me to find you."

Gripping her purse in her lap, Ciara eyed the next set of cars being motioned forward. Another dark two-door was searched; a delivery truck pulled off and was motioned ahead, followed by a red truck.

"We were parked behind that SUV," she said, her heart racing. "You've got to reach him and tell him they're waiting."

A few seconds passed. Suddenly a ferry worker waved his arms wildly, motioning for the police.

"Let's wait at the original rendezvous spot." Dalton put the car in gear and pulled away from the curb.

"You can't leave him," she said.

"I doubt he's still on the ferry."

"What are you talking about?"

"If he's as good as I think he is, he sensed the welcoming party and figured a way to get off the ferry unnoticed."

"You don't know that for sure."

"I know Griffin Black."

He pulled into a parking lot, backed up into a spot in the far corner, out of sight. "We'll wait here."

"For what?"

"Black. He'll show up."

"But everyone's looking for a tall, blue-eyed murder suspect." Her shoulders sagged. "And his female hostage."

"Yeah, we're going to have to do something about that."

"What to you mean?"

"Stay here. Don't get out of the car, got it?"

"Where are you going?"

"Look, Griff trusted me enough to look out for you. Now you need to trust me, okay? I'll be right back."

He locked the car and went into the store. Ciara wondered if the media was airing photos of her and Griff on the late-night news. Who on earth would report Griff as a murderer? His enemies, that's who. Possibly the guy she chased over the cliff into Puget Sound? Yeah, he could have climbed up, called the cops and given them the description of Griff. If the cops detained him, the attacker would have easy access to Ciara.

If the news reported Ciara as a hostage, Adele must be going out of her mind back in Bellevue. No, with any luck, Adele was already tucked safely into bed, missing the late-night news reports.

"Now you're getting ahead of yourself," Ciara whispered. After all just because *shots fired* was reported to Port Townsend police, that didn't mean the media was notified.

She turned up the scanner to hear news about Griff but dreaded it, as well. She couldn't stand the thought of losing him to this violence.

Losing him? Drat, she'd developed feelings for the guy. She couldn't deny it.

"We've apprehended him," a voice said over the scanner. She held her breath. Griff.

"No," she whispered.

"We're bringing him to the station."

Damn, had they apprehended Griff on the way to meet her and Dalton? She opened her car door and got out, straining to see past the roadblock, to see Griff.

"Get back in the car," Dalton ordered, tossing a bag into the backseat.

"But I heard—"

"Now."

She got in and he locked the doors.

"The scanner, they said...they found him, they're taking him in," she said.

"Calm down."

"He can't go to jail. The police can't protect him from the bad guys."

Keen eyed her. "Is he as attached to you as you are to him? Because if that's the case we're screwed."

"What are you talking about?"

"Nothing messes with an agent's focus more than getting personally involved with a mark. Tell me he's not personally involved with you and your problems."

"You don't think I should be grateful to the man who saved my life when I didn't even know I was in danger?"

"Grateful is one thing..." He tapped the steering wheel. "You've gone beyond grateful. I hear it in your voice."

She fumed that he was making her feel guilty about her feelings for Griff. "How long are we going to wait here?"

"As long as it takes."

Not too long, she hoped, or she'd go nuts. How could that be? She actually felt more grounded running from murders than sitting in this car. Why?

Because when she was on the run she was with Griff. There was a confidence about him, a level of integrity that she suspected he'd never admit to having himself.

"You have to do something to help him," she said.

He checked his cell phone and glanced in his rear-view mirror, ignoring her.

"Call your boss," she protested. "Tell him we need more help, that Griff needs help."

"I have my orders."

He shoved the car into gear and they pulled out of the lot.

"You're going to leave him behind?" she said.

He turned up the radio. She talked louder, lecturing him on loyalty and duty and friendship. It felt cathartic to release the anger bottled up inside: anger at faceless terrorists, Gran's criminal ways, even anger at Griff for disappearing on her.

There. That was the crux of it. She'd been abandoned

again by someone she cared about. Yet it hadn't been his choice. He'd been betrayed by one of his own.

Hating the sight of Dalton Keen, she crossed her arms over her chest, feeling so utterly alone.

"You actually stopped. Amazing," Dalton said.

His wisecrack got her going all over again. She turned to him. "Listen, jerk, that guy you left behind was a helluva lot nicer and better at his job than you are. He wouldn't have left you behind."

An odd expression creased his features as he glanced at a patrol car cruising past. "You're absolutely right."

"Then let's go back and save him," she said.

"What, you going to do that? Walk up and blink those sweet green eyes of yours at the cops and ask to take Griff home with you? Lady, it doesn't work like that."

"Yeah, then how does it work? You betray your agent friend to keep your own job?"

"That's enough. You're going to have to trust that I know what I'm doing."

"Do I have a choice?" She stared out the opposite window.

She was done arguing with him, for now. But she wasn't done trying to figure out a way to help Griff. Sure, what could a fragile thing like Ciara do? She cursed her own inexperience.

They drove a good ten minutes in silence, then pulled up to a gate that read Fort Worden State Park. Even in the dark she could make out rows of official-looking buildings.

"What's this place?" she said.

"Oh, so you're talking to me now?" he teased. "This fort, along with two others, guarded against enemy vessels through two world wars. The three forts were called 'Triangle of Fire.' Now it's a state park."

He pulled up beside a gray row house. "Here's home." He grabbed the bag from the backseat and got out. She automatically started for the stairs, but he didn't follow. Instead, he went to the trunk.

"I've got something for you in here," Dalton said.

With an aggravated sigh, she walked up beside him and he unlocked it.

Her heart skipped a beat as she looked down into Griff's blue eyes. Joy rushed to her cheeks. As Dalton helped Griff out she stood there, speechless, trying to process what had happened and how he'd ended up in the trunk.

Then she realized it didn't matter. He was safe. She wrapped her arms around him and squeezed. "You're soaked," she said, but didn't care a bit.

Griff winced. "Careful, there. Remember the gunshot wound."

Ciara stepped back and put out her hands. "Right, I'm so sorry. How did you get in the trunk? They were looking for you. Cops were everywhere and I thought—"

"Shh." Griff put his arm around her and pulled her to his chest, ignoring Dalton's look of disapproval.

"I sensed something was up, so I slipped into the water, sneaked along the shoreline and climbed into Dalton's trunk."

"Your gunshot wound," Ciara said, pulling the jacket away from his shoulder. "We need a doctor."

"First we need to get inside." Dalton led them into the back of the house.

Ciara took Griff's hand, the warmth easing the pain of his festering wound. Griff didn't miss the message in the other agent's raised brow. Ciara had developed an inappropriate attachment to Griff. Like either Griff or Dalton would know *healthy* if they saw it?

Ciara stuck close, as if fearing he'd disappear again, and a part of him appreciated her concern. They stepped into a kitchen with dated metal cabinets and vinyl flooring.

"It's not fancy, but everything works," Dalton said. "There's a bathroom down here and one upstairs. I put fresh towels in both. There are two bedrooms upstairs."

"I'll take the sofa," Griff offered.

"You most certainly will not," Ciara countered. "You're hurt. I'll take the sofa."

"While you two fight over sleeping arrangements, I'll call Doc Winters to have him take a look at your gunshot wound." Dalton sat at the kitchen table and made the call.

Griff followed Ciara into the modest living room. "This isn't bad," she said.

"Glad you like it. You're staying here until we know it's safe for you to reenter society."

"You make it sound like I'm a psychotic mental patient."

"You know what I mean."

She walked to the window and gazed outside. "You think that will ever happen? Will I ever be safe?"

There, she'd finally asked the question. She'd accepted the fact that the smuggling business had irrevocably changed her life.

He should lie to her, tell her everything would be fine and her life would get back to normal in a few weeks. He'd lied before to achieve his goal, placate a mark.

She turned to him, her green eyes red with fatigue. Lying was the best gift he could give her right now. He walked to her side and cupped her chin. "This mission will end and you'll be safe."

How the hell was he going to keep that promise?

"And you'll be where? Saving some other damsel in distress?"

"I'll be doing my job, keeping the citizens of our country safe."

"Why?"

"Someone has to do it."

"Why you? What made you get into this?"

With a reluctant smile, he turned and went to the couch. "Duty was always important in my family: my father was military, as was my brother. Then, after September 11th, it took on a new meaning."

She sat beside him and waited.

"I lost my sister that day," he said.

"Beth," she said.

He nodded.

"I'm so sorry."

"Yeah, well, you expect to lose friends, even relatives in the line of duty, but not like that. It was so—" He paused. "Random. That's why this particular mission drives me insane. The thought of microchips being used to kill innocent people burns like acid on my skin. I guess it makes me act like a madman."

He hoped his explanation would rationalize some of his cruel behavior toward her during the last few days.

"Doc's on his way," Dalton said, coming into the room. "Want some water?" He looked at Griff. "Or whiskey?"

"I'd love a shot."

Dalton looked at Ciara.

"Water would be great," she said.

Dalton disappeared in the kitchen.

"You want to wash up or something?" Griff asked. He could use a few minutes alone with Dalton.

"Yeah, I think that's a good idea," she said.

"Go on. I'll be here when you're done."

"You'd better be." She planted a kiss on his cheek, grabbed her purse and went upstairs.

Dalton came back with two glasses and Ciara's bottled water in the crook of his arm. He handed Griff his shot, placed Ciara's bottle on the coffee table and took a sip of his own drink.

"She's cute," he said, sitting across from Griff in a rocking chair.

"Don't get any ideas," Griff warned.

"I'm not going to steal your girl."

"She's not my girl."

"Uh-huh." He finished his shot.

"You know how these things work. One minute you're strangers, the next you're clinging to each other, running from killers."

"Well, my friend, you saved my life six months ago, now it's my turn to return the favor. Detach from her as soon as possible, and not just for her own good. You know it's impossible to have a relationship with a woman and not put her in danger every minute of every day. But besides that, distance yourself for your own sanity. Women have this power that makes us lose our senses. You lose it for one second and you're dead. Got me?"

"Yes. I appreciate what you're saying."

"But you think I'm full of it."

"No." Griff sipped his drink. "Everything you're saying makes complete sense."

"Good."

"But since when did the world make sense?"

"That's our job," Dalton said. "To make order out of chaos."

"Is that what you call it?"

"Why? What would you call it?"

He leaned back, letting the liquor settle across his shoulders. "I'm starting to think, for me, it's about easing my guilt over something completely out of my control."

"You've got control over this thing, Griff. Don't lose it and get yourself killed over a woman."

"Good advice, thanks."

"Listen, we'd better work on your looks in case you're spotted. Time for a military shave, my friend. I've got a spare set of contacts and clothes. Bought hair color for Ciara, too."

"The good kind, I hope."

"What do you mean?"

"I made her use shoe polish to darken it."

"Creative. What about your car? Can they trace it?"

"No, it's registered to Manny Durge of St. Louis. My prints are untraceable."

A knock sounded from the front door. Griff reached for his firearm, but Dalton waved him off.

"It's probably Doc Winters. Be nice to him. We interrupted his star gazing."

"You're kidding me."

"Nope," Dalton shrugged. "He's quirky but trustworthy."

"You sure he's on our side?"

"He's a good guy, just a little beaten up by the business." Dalton opened the door.

"What the hell?" a fortyish man said, racing into the room and slamming the door. "The place is crawling with cops."

Chapter Eleven

"Upstairs on the right," Dalton ordered Griff. "There's a crawl space in my bedroom."

Griff stood and hissed against the pain.

"I'd better look at that." Doc Winters took a step toward him.

"Later. Keep watch out the front window while I'll get him upstairs." Dalton put Griff's arm around his shoulder.

"I can walk by myself," Griff said, but the sudden movement shot pain down his arm.

"Yeah, well, you'll move faster if I help you."

They went upstairs, Griff feeling as worthless as an empty M4 Carbine rifle.

"Ciara, get in here, now!" Dalton ordered.

She came out of the bathroom drying her hands on a towel. "What is it?"

"Cops. We need to hide you two in case they search the place. Grab your stuff."

Dalton led Griff to a paneled wall and opened a door. "There's a lock on the inside and outside," Dalton said. "Lock yourself in. I'll tell them it's been jammed shut ever since I moved in."

Ciara didn't move. "I…" She glanced at Griff and he read her thoughts. She was starting to panic.

"It's okay. You can do this," he said.

"What if they find us and…and arrest us?" Ciara asked, probably stalling so she didn't have to go into the closet. "The cops can't protect us from the terrorists. Officer Banks is a cop and he's one of the bad guys."

"Would you shut her up and get her inside?" Dalton said to Griff.

"They won't find us," Griff assured. "They may not even search the house." He extended his hand and Ciara automatically reached for it, as if they'd touched and held each other a thousand times.

"Ladies first," he said, keeping the concern from his voice. She was right. If the cops took them into custody, they were toast.

Griff led her into the storage closet. "You're going to be fine. I'm here."

Dalton poked his head inside. "I'll do my best to keep them from coming upstairs."

He shut the door and Griff locked it from the inside. She snuggled against his chest and a moan escaped his lips at the warm contact.

She jerked back. "Did I hurt you?"

"No, you're fine."

She was more than fine. She was warm and soft, and the one thing that grounded him right now. Hell, if they were discovered at least he would have had the pleasure of holding this beautiful woman in his arms before being dragged off to a holding cell and sure death.

No, they wouldn't be found. Dalton would make sure of it. Still, Dalton had gotten into his previous mess because he trusted the wrong person. What if he'd made the same mistake with the doctor downstairs?

Couldn't think about that now. Had to focus on being invisible.

A skill he'd perfected. Being invisible and nonexistent.

Except he didn't feel nonexistent with Ciara clinging to him. He felt powerful and alive.

"Do you think they followed us here?" she whispered.

"Not likely. Dalton has a solid cover. There'd be no reason to suspect him. This is probably a general canvas of town."

"I heard them talking over the scanner," she said. "They arrested someone they thought was you."

"They've probably figured out they've got the wrong guy."

A few minutes passed. Griff focused on the activity downstairs but heard nothing, no knock on the door, no male conversation.

"Griff?"

"Yeah?"

"What do we do next?"

"Stay alive."

CIARA closed her eyes at his admission. He'd been the strong one, confident and determined that they'd claw their way out of this mess and past the danger that awaited them around every corner.

But in his answer she heard both determination and resignation. They'd be hunted until the bad guys found the chips, and even then they'd probably kill her and Griff because of their involvement.

Breathing against Griff's cotton shirt, she took comfort in his strength. She hadn't missed Dalton's look before, the one that shamed Griff for caring too much about her. The odd thing was even though Griff hid behind a shield of deception, there was something very real, very authentic about this man who sacrificed his life to save innocents. She suspected even he didn't recognize that authenticity anymore.

"I'm sorry," she said.

"For what?"

"That you were shot because of me."

"I was shot because of the job."

"Yeah, tracking criminals like my grandmother."

"I'm sorry about that, Ciara, truly."

As they sat in complete darkness, she brushed her fingertips against his cheek and he leaned into her touch.

"You have nothing to be sorry about," she said. "Gran, on the other hand, was smuggling weapons to be used against her own country."

The chime of a doorbell echoed. "Griff," she said, clutching his shirt.

"Shh." He cradled her face in his hand and guided it to his chest. "Focus on my heartbeat."

Clutching his shirt, she closed her eyes and did as he asked, ignoring the male voices downstairs. She couldn't imagine living like this indefinitely, yet she knew that was a distinct possibility. After all, even if they caught the terrorist agents who pursued Griff and Ciara, that didn't guarantee more wouldn't come looking for her, looking for contraband she couldn't give them.

Footsteps pounded up the stairs.

"Shh. It's going to be okay," he whispered.

Focusing on his heartbeat, she let the outside world drift away, pretending this was a bad dream, one she could push aside for the promise of something wonderful.

She couldn't remember the last time she thought the word *wonderful*. She'd been so consumed with making Gran's business a success. An illegal business that had taken over her life as she struggled to come up with creative ways to increase profit and decrease expenses.

The same business that could very well cause her death.

"You can search the entire house, but I've been here most of the night and I'd know if someone broke in," Dalton said from the other side of the door.

This was it. She was going to be taken in, found by terrorists and killed. Suddenly she wanted to fight, right the wrongs of her grandmother.

As male voices drifted through the door she prayed they wouldn't be found. She wanted another chance to follow her own dreams instead of giving her life away to someone else's, to a criminal's.

Please, God. Please don't let them find us.

Someone rattled the door. Griff held her close and she took a deep breath. She could do this, she could make it past the panic because Griff was holding her.

"You have a key to this?" a man said.

"Nope," Dalton answered. "The property manager said it's been lost for years. Too bad. I could use the storage space."

Silence. Another jiggle.

Griff stroked Ciara's hair in a rhythmic movement, grounding her, easing the panic attack threatening to take hold.

She'd be okay. Griff was here, comforting her, protecting her.

"Why are you guys searching my place?" Dalton asked.

"A murder suspect got off the ferry tonight," a deep voice answered through the door. "This park is a great place to disappear with all the campsites, rentals and hiking trails."

"Yeah, good point."

"You've got a good view from this bedroom," a man said. "I heard you were in the military—Special Forces."

"Yes, sir, that is true."

"I'd appreciate it if you kept an eye out for the suspect and the hostage. If you see anything suspicious I'd appreciate a call."

"Of course you can count on my help," Dalton said.

The voices grew farther away. Footsteps thumped down the stairs and a door slammed.

The danger had passed. They were going to be okay for now. She couldn't wait for Dalton to give them the official All Clear signal. She needed out.

She unlocked the door and pushed it open. "Griff, let's go." She glanced over her shoulder. Light from the bedroom streamed across his pale face. He was unconscious. Or was he dead?

"Griff, no." She gently tapped his cheek, but he didn't respond. She pressed her ear to his chest, just as he'd asked her to do before. *Focus on my heartbeat.* But her adrenaline was rushing so fast that she couldn't hear anything past her own racing heartbeat.

"Help! Dalton, get up here!" she cried, trying to pull Griff out into the open.

Feet pounded up the stairs. "I said to stay inside." Dalton rounded the corner and eyed Griff's limp body. "Doc!" he called over his shoulder, then went to Griff's side. "He just passed out?" Dalton asked, hoisting Griff to the bed.

"Yes."

"Stay back," he said to Ciara.

Guilt tore her apart. No matter how many times Griff said he was shot because of his job, Ciara blamed herself. The shooter had been after her, her dolls and the microchips.

"I don't want anyone outside to see you," he said, pulling the shades.

The doctor came into the room. "What happened?"

"He was talking and holding me and then nothing," she explained.

The doctor placed his backpack of supplies next to the bed. "You be my assistant," he said to Dalton.

"What can I do?" Ciara asked.

"Stay out of the way."

She tried not to take the comment personally, but it sounded like he blamed her for Griff's condition. Hadn't she just done the same thing?

Dr. Winters took Griff's pulse and searched his eyes with a penlight.

"What's his name?" the doctor asked.

"Griff," Ciara offered.

"Griffin Black," Dalton added.

"Griffin Black, can you hear me?" the doctor said.

No response.

"I'm treating him for shock." He dug his keys from his pocket and tossed them at Dalton. "There's an IV of saline in my car."

Dalton went downstairs, leaving Ciara alone with the doctor.

"So, you two playing kissy face in there?" he said, listening to Griff's chest.

She didn't know what to say.

He analyzed Griff's injury, peeling the bandage off the wound and making a face.

"I did the best I could," she defended, pacing the room. "Can you fix him?"

"He's a human being, not a clock radio."

"I got it!" Dalton said, coming into the room with the IV bag.

Doctor Winters set up the bag and inserted a needle in Griff's arm.

"What's that?" Ciara asked.

"Get her out of here," the doctor said to Dalton.

"I'll stop pacing," she said.

"I need her out," the man said, focused on cleansing the wound.

Dalton escorted her into the hallway. "He's got no social skills, but he's a good doctor. Wait in the spare bedroom. I'll let you know when you can see him."

She appreciated the comforting tone, even if she sensed he was lying. He didn't know for a fact Griff would be okay. As she headed into the spare room, she felt so alone. Both the doctor and Dalton treated her like an irritating child, and if anything happened to Griff…

She considered life without him. It looked dismal. Heavens, how had he become such an important part of her life in a matter of days? It reminded her of the kind of mental condition that hostages experienced. Stockholm syndrome.

But how could she break free of it? Get her perspective back? She scanned the bookcase, looking for something to divert her attention. She plucked a history text from the shelf and cracked it open. Who was she kidding? Like she could think about anything but the man in the next room fighting for his life?

A few minutes later Dalton came to see her. "He seems better."

She jumped to her feet.

"The doc says no visitors for a few hours."

"Now wait a second—"

"He needs to stay calm." Dalton stepped into the room and closed the door. "Look, Ciara, Griff needs to take care of himself right now and if he hears your voice or senses your presence, he'll feel compelled to take care of you. Just—" He paused. "Give him some space, okay?"

She sat down on the bed. "You think I'd aggravate his condition?"

"It's the way he is, always putting his job first, especially before himself. Let's not tempt him. Let him rest. The doctor will sit with him for an hour, and I'll take over. Maybe if his blood pressure stabilizes, you can take the third shift. Sound good?"

"Sure, thanks."

"You need anything? Food, water?"

"Sounds like I'm in jail."

"It's not that bad. The previous tenant left a nice book collection, if you're into that kind of thing."

She suspected Dalton Keen was not a big reader.

"Thanks, I noticed."

"Well, you know where the bathroom is. I'll come by when it's your shift."

"Okay, thanks."

"Do you know where the microchips are?"

"In Griff's front pocket." And once they were handed off, she'd be handed off, as well.

DALTON shut the door on the woman's lost expression. He'd have to immunize himself from it if she was to be a permanent resident for the next few months.

He went into Griff's room and shut the door. Doc

Winters sighed and wrapped the stethoscope around his neck. Old habits died hard. Although the doc was demoted to shrink for AW-21 misfits, he still acted like a chief surgeon on rounds.

"He needs to be in a hospital," the doc said.

"Can't do it. The gunshot wound would draw attention."

"Who's after him, anyway?"

"Actually, they're after the woman."

"He took a bullet for *her?* She's not worth it."

"How would you know? You've barely talked to her."

"I know women. They're not worth it."

Dalton couldn't disagree. A woman had betrayed him on his mission, quite possibly his last in the field.

"Regardless," Dalton said. "Griff was following orders. She had something the government wants."

"Don't tell me. I'm retired." He plopped down in the chair next to the bed. "Go on. I'll watch him for a bit."

"Before I forget." Dalton reached into Griff's front pocket for the microchips, but both pockets were empty.

"You looking for this?" Doc Winters held up a vial with two small chips.

"Yeah, thanks." Dalton reached for it, but Doc snatched it back.

"What's it worth to you?" Doc said, stepping toward the door.

"That isn't funny."

"I'm not laughing."

"Doc, give me the chips." For a second he wondered if he'd been played again, if Doc was a spy for the other side. Then he noticed that lost look in Doc's eyes.

"Don't you get it, Keen? We've got the power here.

We've got the weapon everyone wants to get their hands on."

Dalton fisted and unfisted his hand, trying to control the urge to lunge across the bed and strangle the guy. "Whose side are you on, Doc?"

"Our side, Keen." He eyed the vial. "We could finally be free of these bastards, cut off their chains of service. Tell them we'll give up the chips for a million bucks and an honorable discharge."

The guy had spent too much time alone in this remote corner of the country. "They'd hunt us down and kill us and that's if we turned over the microchips," Dalton said.

"Then we keep them, for insurance."

"Doc," Keen warned.

"Damn it, you were sent to this solitary hell because of them. I'm stuck playing grounds supervisor and going out of my mind. Your friend here is going to die because they've set him up like a duck in an arcade game. And you, you ever think you'll see active duty again?"

"It doesn't matter."

"Like hell it doesn't. I've seen you wandering the grounds, pulling out your binoculars to watch the ships pass through. I know that look. You'd do anything to be on one of those ships sailing the hell out of here. You need back into action. You need to kick some ass."

Right now he wanted to kick Doc's ass.

"There is a bigger picture here, Doc."

"The bigger picture is we're all going to die. I want to die rich and free."

He pulled a small pistol from the inside pocket of his jacket. The guy was completely losing it. Dalton knew the feeling, only he'd had his mental meltdown in private with a bottle of whiskey.

Although the guy's breakdown didn't surprise Dalton, he didn't appreciate the timing. The last thing he wanted to do was neutralize the one guy who could save Griff's life.

"I could have been a great doctor," Doc said, edging toward the door. "I could have saved lives."

"You still can. What you've got in your hand is designed to kill innocent people. You don't want it out in circulation."

"No, but these would be worth a lot to our own, pathetic government."

"That's not freedom, Doc. That's blackmail."

"Call it whatever you want. I can't stand it anymore, can't stand being invisible, nonexistent, being nothing."

"I don't have to take orders from you," Ciara said, swinging open the door.

It slammed into Doc, who accidentally fired a shot.

Ciara shrieked.

Dalton lunged for the weapon, shoving back the thought that the bullet might have hit Griff.

Chapter Twelve

Dalton shouldered Ciara into the wall as he charged the doctor. She caught her breath and pushed past them, rushing to protect Griff. Yeah, like she was made of bulletproof armor or something.

Dalton snatched the gun from the doctor and stepped back, waving it in his face. "What the hell's the matter with you?"

With shallow, adrenaline-charged breaths, Ciara searched Griff's body, but he hadn't been hit. Relieved, she got in the doctor's face.

"You're a doctor. You're supposed to heal people, not kill them. What were you thinking?"

He stared at Griff, as if the reality of what he'd done just hit him. He slid down the wall and sat on the floor, burying his face in his hands.

"They've done this," he whispered. "They made me into a killer."

"Come on," Dalton helped him back up. "You need a drink."

"A drink?" Ciara said. "He almost killed Griff and you're offering him a drink?"

"Let it go." Dalton glared at her. "You're judging something you can't possibly understand."

She started to argue, but Griff moaned behind her.

"Take care of Griff," Dalton said to her.

"Take care of him how? What can I do?" She kneeled beside him and held his hand.

"It doesn't matter," the doctor said. "He's going to die. We're all going to die."

"Downstairs." Dalton shoved the doctor into the hallway and glanced at Ciara. "Talk to him. Let him hear the sound of your voice."

Dalton closed the door. The room was incredibly silent, the crack of the gunshot still ringing in her ears. She brought Griff's hand to her lips and whispered, "It's going to be okay."

Her chest ached with the lie. These men lived violent, tumultuous lives. How could it ever be okay?

A moan rumbled against his throat.

"Shh, Griff, you're okay. You're safe."

She noticed he stirred when she didn't talk to him, so she kept rambling.

"Remember when we first met?" she started. "You were studying a doll, trying to figure out why people are so enamored with them? You were commenting on the doll's eyes and I couldn't stop looking at yours..."

She'd keep talking until his anxious sleep passed, sleep probably filled with memories of past missions, lost loves and most certainly his lost sister.

"And you were such a gentleman, so polite and charming. Adele wanted me to get back on the horse and flirt with you, but I'm not the flirting type, not really. Then you came into the gift shop and I was so embarrassed that you caught me dressing up. My whole life

I'd dreamed of being glamorous, instead of a carrot top. It's funny the things we dream about, isn't it? I wish you'd wake up and tell me about your dreams. Please wake up, Griff. Please wake up."

THE SWEET, tender voice drifted to him from the far corners of his mind, enchanting and beguiling, yet humming with desperation.

It wasn't Beth, a voice he'd heard often in his dreams. It was *her* voice, the goddess of his dreams, an angel who was calling to him, guiding him when he didn't think he could find his way.

The sweet sound echoed through his ears to his mind and down to wrap around his heart. She was showing him the way, leading him out of the darkness, past anchored resentment and guilt over his failures.

And there, as he looked up…was the light.

Griff opened his eyes and blinked a few times to register his surroundings. Sunlight peered through a crack in an old white shade. Where was he again?

"You're awake." Dalton Keen came into view. "How do you feel?"

"Tired."

"Your blood pressure dropped. Doc got some fluids and antibiotics into you." He nodded at the IV. "You look like a new man."

"Gee, thanks."

"She talked to you all night, hoping it would bring you back."

That's when Griff felt Ciara against him, her arm flung protectively across his chest.

"Looks like it worked," Dalton said.

"I heard her voice. I thought it was…" He hesitated.

"An angel?" Dalton offered a knowing smile.

Apparently Griff wasn't the only one who communed with angels when he thought he was about to die.

"Do you remember the excitement last night?" Dalton asked.

"The cops?"

"You don't remember anything else?"

"No, what did I miss?"

"Doc had a moment. Thought he could buy his freedom from AW-21 by stealing the microchips."

Griff started to sit up, but Dalton placed his hand to his shoulder. "I've got 'em. We're good. But I think the doc needs a mental tune-up."

"What day is it again?"

"Friday."

"We're losing time. It goes into the engine on Monday."

"You need to recover."

"No time for that. What's the status of the packages?"

"They've been flagged, so they'll be held by local authorities until we get to them. Relax, it's under control. What did you want me to do with these two?" He pulled the small tube from his pocket.

"We've got to get them to D.C."

"CO Andrews has other agents in the area. Should we ask him to assign someone to take it back?"

"I should be the one," Griff said.

"You're not up to it. I told Andrews about your gunshot wound, that you could use a little time to recover."

"You shouldn't have done that."

"Sure I should. It's not like you'd intentionally take care of yourself." He eyed Ciara. "You want me to pull her off of you?"

Dalton could pull Ciara off of Griff, but it wouldn't matter. She'd worked her way into his heart.

"No, she's fine," Griff said.

"Uh-huh. That's one word for it."

"I'm going to need your help with this one." He eyed her.

"You mean when you have to leave her in Port Townsend?"

"Yes."

"I'm not sure this is the safest place now that they're looking for you."

"It'll have to be safe until I can get her into the WD program."

"Good luck with that," Dalton said.

Witness disappearance was AW-21's version of witness protection, but harder to get into.

"She's saved my life multiple times and has helped track down the chips," Griff said. "I won't let them abandon her to our enemies."

"How far are you willing to go on this?"

"It's a deal breaker."

The words shocked even Griff. He'd walk away from the agency in order to protect Ciara? Yep, he would. He simply couldn't stand sacrificing this innocent beauty who had so much to offer the world.

And Griff.

"You want me to bring it up with Andrews?" Dalton said.

"No. I'll do it. Where's my phone?"

Dalton grabbed it from the dresser and handed it to him. "Hell, give yourself a day off. Nothing's going to happen to the girl in the next twenty-four hours." He went to the door and turned. "Listen, I was wondering if you'd want me to go to Seattle for the packages."

"You're on leave."

"Yeah, well, I'm hoping that by helping you out I could earn points to get me back into the field. I mean, you need to recover and you'd be doing me a big favor."

"That's two," he joked.

"Bad idea, huh?"

"No, not bad. Let's talk later."

"Okay, sure. I'll make some eggs or something. Want me to bring it upstairs?"

"No, we'll be down in a bit."

Dalton nodded and closed the door.

In the past Griff had never considered abandoning his primary mission, but Dalton's offer was tempting, especially if it meant Griff could spend another day or two with Ciara.

Yes, the sooner he separated from her the better. She'd bewitched him somehow and he'd never be able to think straight with her near him.

"What's a WD program?" she said.

"You're awake?"

She leaned on an upturned palm and eyed him. Even first thing in the morning her emerald eyes sparkled with color.

"I was waking up and didn't want to interrupt."

"You were eavesdropping, naughty girl."

"Sorry. But I get the feeling you keep things from me to protect me, so if I'm a fly on the wall I'll find out what's really going on."

He was about to protest that he'd always been truthful with her, but they both knew that wasn't true.

"So, what's WD?" she pushed.

"It's our version of witness protection."

"In other words, I'd be sent away, give up my life, my friends, and start all over?"

"Yes."

She thought for a moment. "Sounds great."

"It does?"

"Sure, my current life is nothing but a lie. I'd recreate myself and no one would know I'm the granddaughter of a smuggler working with terrorists."

She liked the idea. Relief washed over Griff. She'd be safe.

"Griff, did you hear me, before?" she whispered. "I talked to you all night or at least until I fell asleep."

Griff closed his eyes. Sure, he'd heard the whispers of encouragement that brought him back from the darkness.

Darkness. All he had to offer her. She deserved more.

"I heard you," he said. "Thanks."

"What now?"

"How about breakfast?"

"I meant about the terrorists who are after us?"

"We're safe here. Let's enjoy the moment, relax a bit."

But he wouldn't relax until he'd gotten her safely into the program and walked away.

Never to see her again.

GRIFF welcomed the mid-morning meal, a reprieve from the stress of the last few days. Griff, Ciara and Dalton sat at the kitchen table, eating eggs and toast and drinking really bad coffee. Ciara had showered, put up her hair and changed into an oversize T-shirt that doubled as a dress.

"We need to get you more clothes," Griff said, gripping his shoulder.

"Are you in pain?" she questioned, leaning forward in her chair.

"Not bad."

"I've got painkillers," Dalton said, going to the cupboard. "Oh, and didn't Doc leave a sling?"

"Yeah, hang on." Ciara raced upstairs and came back a minute later with a black sling. She tied it around Griff's neck and adjusted his arm to rest against his chest.

"Doc should be bringing by some fresh clothes for you, Ciara."

"You let him wander the streets?" she asked. "He's a lunatic."

Dalton sat at the table and slid a bottle of aspirin across to Griff. "Doc's going through some posttraumatic challenges."

"He shouldn't be allowed to carry a gun," she said.

"Yeah, I think he knows that now," Dalton said.

"What did I miss?" Griff asked.

"Never mind," Dalton said. "Look, the ferry leaves in two hours for Seattle. I can catch it, pick up the packages and analyze them on the spot. I'll find the chip, report in and it's all over."

"I should really be the one to finish the mission," Griff said.

"And I should have been the one to rescue the Anders girl, but I screwed up and you saved my butt. Time for me to return the favor. You stay here and recuperate while I wrap it up."

"Did you check this with CO Andrews?"

"I was waiting on your answer."

Griff glanced at Ciara who leveled him with pleading green eyes. Truth was, he wouldn't mind another day to recover. Or was it that he craved more time with Ciara because he knew their time together was coming to an end?

"Okay," Griff said. "Run it past Andrews."

Ciara smiled and sipped her coffee.

Dalton grabbed his cell phone and called in, walking out the back door for privacy. Or was it to give him and Ciara privacy, so Griff could clarify his purpose for letting Dalton take over? It couldn't be because Griff wanted to pursue a relationship with Ciara. For God's sake, neither of them was in a place to have a relationship beyond running from danger.

"Thanks," Ciara said, but didn't look at him.

"For what?"

"For agreeing to play protector for a little while longer."

"Is that what I am?" He smiled.

He realized he was flirting with her, but in a sweet way, so unlike his usual style. It was his style to buy a woman a drink or two, compliment her eyes and hair, then take her to bed.

"Yep, you're my protector," she said.

"What does that make you?"

"Your nurse." She winked.

He rethought the wisdom of letting Dalton leave them alone. At least with the other agent in the house, Griff couldn't ignore his conscience.

Dalton reentered the kitchen. "The CO says it's a go. You stay back and I'll take it from here. I mentioned the WD program. Said he'd look into it and call you later. He was going into a meeting."

"Great, thanks."

"I've gotta get organized." Dalton breezed out of the kitchen and raced up the stairs.

"He's awfully excited," Ciara said.

"He loves his work, being out in the field, I mean."

"Is that your favorite part, too?" She nibbled on a piece of toast.

"I guess."

"What else do you like about your work? You mentioned travel and not being tied down before."

Did he even know? He'd thrown himself into the job to feel better about not being able to save his sister. But recently he'd started to question his selfless act. He'd given his life over to the agency, had become another person, a ghost, who didn't exist.

Until this sweet girl was dropped into his life.

"Wow," she said, studying him. "I didn't know it was such a tough question."

He forked his eggs, but didn't eat.

"Let me rephrase. Is it worth it? Is being a spy or whatever you call yourself, worth giving up everything else?"

"I used to think so," Griff said. "But lately I'm just tired. Maybe I need a break."

"Or a new life."

THERE, she'd tossed out the challenge. Maybe she wasn't the only one who needed a change of identity program. Maybe Griff needed to be sent to a place to recover and rebuild, and maybe he'd come back in another, less threatening role for the government.

"What would you suggest I do, Miss O'Malley?"

"Well, you've got natural charm. You could be a salesman."

"And sell what? Vacuums?"

"Ladies' shoes."

He chuckled. "Why shoes?"

"Or anything to do with selling to women. It's the blue eyes, they're hypnotic."

"You mean I could convince a woman to do anything just by looking at her?"

"Pretty much."

He leaned forward across the table. "Then kiss me."

And without hesitation, she did. His lips parted for her and she couldn't help but deepen the kiss. So gentle and warm. So perfect.

Suddenly, Griff pulled away, his expression dark and confused.

"What? You asked me to," she said.

"I was kidding."

"Oh." She leaned back and sipped her coffee. She'd secretly wanted to kiss him since the first time they'd met at the museum. She usually didn't fantasize about strange men, but Griff's eyes called out to her, both the amazing sea blue color and the vulnerability behind them.

"I'm sorry," he said. "I've hurt your feelings."

"No, I'm embarrassed. I thought you wanted me to kiss you. I'm silly."

She stood, took his plate and hers and went to the sink.

"Ciara—"

"Doc's pulling up," Dalton called from the front room.

"Great, I'll get some real clothes." Ciara turned to Griff and smiled, trying to hide her feelings. A man like Griff wasn't into plain, naive women. He'd probably had tons of exotic, powerful ones in his bed.

Dalton poked his head into the kitchen. "Aren't you going to come see what he got you?"

"Sure." Ciara rinsed the plates and put them in the dishwasher. She sensed Griff follow close behind her.

He placed his hand to her lower back and she practically melted into the floor.

"You ready?" he said.

Uh, if he only knew.

"Sure." She slipped away from his touch and headed for the living room. "Let's hope it's not more lime-green."

GRIFF couldn't believe how his body came alive from the kiss. He was tired and beaten. That part of his body should not be functional. At all.

Yet watching her get excited about the clothes was turning him on.

Dalton shook his head at Griff, probably thinking Griff had completely lost his perspective and it was a good thing he wasn't going after the chips. His clarity was shot and he'd be worrying about Ciara instead of his primary mission.

A few hours later Dalton left for Seattle, and Ciara changed into something that fit her better, although a little snug. The Doc did the best he could, so Griff didn't hold it against him that he'd bought her tight-fitting T-shirts.

Griff paced to the front window, keeping watch for anything suspicious. Doc said his police buddy heard the suspect and hostage had been seen heading south, toward Tacoma. According to the cop, all search efforts in Port Townsend had ceased.

They were safe for the time being. Dalton was positive that Doc's "moment" was over, that the guy could be trusted. That was good enough for Griff.

"You need to relax," Ciara said, coming up beside him. She'd decided to wear a royal-blue tank top and shorts. He wished she'd put the oversize T-shirt back on.

"What?" she eyed him.

"Nothing."

"Cabin fever already? And we haven't even been cooped up here for twenty-four hours. Let's play a game. I found some cards in the kitchen drawer."

The only card game he could remember was strip poker.

"Or we could talk," she offered.

"Cards."

"Coward." She smiled and got the cards.

Of course he was a coward. He didn't want to share any more of himself with this woman, nor did he want to learn more of her secrets. They'd surely haunt him once she was ripped from his life and he was haunted enough by his own demons. He didn't need more to fight off.

She sat on the sofa and tugged his sleeve to encourage him to join her.

"What's the game?" he said, sitting beside her.

"Blackjack."

"What are we betting?"

"No betting, it's just for fun. I used to play this with my dad when I was little."

"Thanks," he let slip.

She laid a queen on top of his card and glanced up. "For what?"

"For distracting me."

"Is that what I'm doing?" She smiled. "You want me to hit you or do you want to stick?"

She peeked at her facedown card and nibbled her lower lip. He studied his cards, fighting the memory of the taste of those lips.

"I guess you need me to hit you, huh?" she said.

"Yes."

She slapped down another card, but he barely registered it, so caught up in this very normal moment. So this is what it felt like to enjoy a woman's company without having to bed her?

She turned over her own cards and had a nineteen.

"How'd you do?"

He turned over his card and they added up to twenty-five.

"You shouldn't have taken the hit," she said. "Don't you know how to play this game?"

His cell phone vibrated. Good, refocusing on work would distract him from his dangerous thoughts.

"Black." He stood and went to the kitchen.

"Any word from Keen?" his CO asked.

"Not yet, sir. He's in Seattle, waiting for the delivery."

"Have you identified the smuggler?"

"Not yet, sir. I've been more focused on finding the chips."

"I understand you want Ciara O'Malley processed into the WD program?"

"Yes, sir."

"You think she's worth it?"

She was worth it and much more.

"Yes, sir."

"You'll need to transfer her to our Portland location by Tuesday."

Relief washed through him. He thought his CO might reject his request, but he didn't. Ciara would be safe and starting a new life somewhere, the details of which even Griff wouldn't be privy to.

"Thank you, sir."

"What kind of recovery time do you need?"

"A few weeks."

"Once we apprehend the smuggler and recover the chips, plan to take a month off."

"Yes, sir."

"That's all, Lieutenant."

Griff went into the living room and found Ciara playing a card game with the four kings lined up.

"You winning?"

"Don't know yet. I'm telling my fortune." She eyed the deck. "Who's the best kisser?" She flipped over cards until one matched the king of hearts. "Interesting."

"Good news," he said. "You're in the program. Next Tuesday you'll start your new life."

"What's my new name?" she asked.

"I don't know."

"But you will, right?" She leaned back and smiled at him.

"No, Ciara, I won't know your name or where you've been sent or what you'll do for a living."

"I'll never see you again?" She put the cards down.

"No."

"Then I'm not interested."

"Don't be stupid." He sat beside her and grabbed the cards. "This, whatever you think is going on between us, isn't real."

"No? Tell me this isn't real."

And she kissed him.

Chapter Thirteen

Ciara might be a somewhat naive woman, but she knew real emotions when they grabbed hold of her heart. She'd never felt this kind of pull for her former fiancé, or any other man.

His lips were warm and soft, so perfect against hers as she teased at the opening with her tongue.

With firm hands to her shoulders, he broke the kiss. "Stop. Ciara, don't do this."

"You can't tell me you don't feel anything when I kiss you."

"Of course I do. I'm a man. I'm going to have a physical reaction when a woman kisses me." He let go of her and paced to the window.

"It's more than that," she said.

"What do you think it is?" He turned, his eyes midnight-blue. "Love? Is that where you're going with this?"

"Why not?"

"This isn't love. This is Stockholm syndrome. You know what that is?"

"Yes, I do." She crossed her arms over her chest.

"Then you know it's when a hostage develops feelings for her captor. That's what you're experiencing."

"You're not my captor. You're my protector."

"I'm a government agent on a mission to find microchips. Once I accomplish my mission, I'll disappear into a new mission."

"But you don't have to. You could—"

"What, start a life with you?"

"Why not?"

"This isn't real, Ciara. This is my job. My job was to seduce you and get information from you. Seduce you. So while you've concocted this fantasy about your cooking dinner and me going off to work, you think about the other women I'll be seducing in the line of duty."

"Then do something else."

"Not an option."

"Why? What will happen if you quit?"

He put up his index finger to silence her. "Don't."

"They'll find someone else to give up his life, his soul to protect the United States. You're not indispensable, Griff. So why are you afraid to give it up?"

"I'm not afraid."

She got in his face. "Sure you are. You're terrified."

"This conversation is over."

"The hell it is. Tell me what will happen if you quit."

He turned his back, shutting her out.

"Okay, let me figure it out," she said. "I'll bet it has something to do with your sister's death."

He spun and gripped her shoulder. "Drop it."

"Wait a second, I get it. You're sacrificing your life because she lost hers. That's it, isn't it?"

"No."

"You feel guilty? Are you honoring her death by being a spy? By giving up your life and your happiness?"

"I don't deserve happiness." The words slipped off

Griff's tongue and he feared she'd use his confession against him.

"Sure you do. And I'll bet your sister would be devastated if she knew you were giving up your chance at happiness in her name. You're burying yourself in guilt over something you had no control over."

"You don't understand."

"I want to. Explain it to me."

"My sister—" He paused.

Ciara touched his cheek, and he couldn't hold it in anymore.

"Beth was bright and funny and didn't deserve to die." Griff wandered away from her, not wanting to see Ciara's face as he spoke. "She did so much for other people. All I did was think about my own needs, screw off, party my brains out. But she's the one who died because of the crazy bastards who will keep on killing unless I stop them."

"Did you just hear yourself?" She pinned him with her intense green eyes. "You're going to stop them all by yourself?"

"Or die trying."

"That's not honoring your sister's memory, Griff. That's making her a martyr."

Her words smacked him like a two-by-four to the chest. "No, I've been making it safe for people like Beth."

"By sacrificing your own life?" She went to him and placed her open palm to his chest. The contact shot warmth through his shirt to his heart. A loving touch, tender and magical.

He couldn't move.

"Your sister would have wanted you to live a full life, Griff. She'd want you to be happy."

"I don't...I don't remember what that feels like."

"It's something like this." With her hand at the back of his neck, she coaxed him forward.

"Ciara," he breathed in protest just before their lips touched. And once they did, he was lost. His conscience, his better judgment, was obliterated by the hum coursing through his body. It wasn't intense physical desire. It was something else, a connection he'd never felt before.

She was right. They'd developed a strong, unnatural connection in their short time together. But was she also right about his sacrificing his life in his sister's memory instead of honoring her senseless death?

Ciara weaved her fingers through his hair and pulled him even closer, her tongue flirting at the corner of his lips. He grew lightheaded, but not from his injury.

She broke the kiss, took his hand and led him up the stairs with a determined expression.

"Ciara, I may not be up to—"

She pressed her finger to his lips. "No more talking. Just happiness."

CIARA guided him on the bed and kissed his cheek. "Wait here."

She went into Dalton's room and found a condom in the nightstand drawer. She stripped to her bra and panties and tucked the foil packet in her cleavage.

She'd never wanted to seduce a man, pleasure a man like this, but in Griff's arms she wasn't insecure or self-conscious. Even when he'd protested her advances, she didn't take it personally because she knew he cared about her.

And that obviously scared the hell out of him. She read

fear in his eyes, but not fear of her. Fear of hurting her, which was confirmation that he did have feelings for her. Did she even dare say, he was falling in love with her?

Because she knew, deep down, this was a man she could love with all her heart. She hovered in the doorway, half-naked and eyed Griff who was standing by the window.

"Griff?"

He turned, and his eyes widened with desire. She extended her hand, but he hesitated.

"I…you're so beautiful, but this is…dangerous."

"Let me worry about the danger for a while. Please?" She motioned with her hand and he took it, eyeing her curves with appreciation.

"How about you sit on the bed and I'll undress you?" she said.

First, she removed his sling. "How's the shoulder wound?"

"What shoulder wound?"

She smiled, pulled his T-shirt from the waistband of his jeans and slid it up and over his head. Griff studied his hands, folded loosely in his lap as if he felt guilty.

"Look at me," she said.

When he glanced into her eyes, she thought her heart would break. He looked so beaten, so guilty. She was determined to wipe that look off his face. Pushing him back against the bed, she unzipped his jeans and slid them off. It was obvious that even if his mind protested her advances, his body was willing and more than able to experience the magic shared between a man and woman.

She started by nuzzling his cheek and working her way down his neck laying gentle kisses against his skin.

"You are an amazing man," she said. "You deserve to be blissfully happy."

As she nuzzled her way down his lightly-haired chest she felt his hands cup and squeeze her shoulders. She slid her hand down, brushing against his boxers.

"Ciara." It was a low, rumbling sound from deep in his chest.

She straddled him and arched, his manhood teasing her from beneath his cotton underwear.

"You're a witch," he hissed.

She leaned forward, brushing the tips of her breasts against his chest.

"This needs to be off." With one hand he removed her bra and the condom packet dropped to his chest. "For me?" he said, leaning forward to taste her. His warm, moist tongue grazed her nipple and she automatically arched for him.

"Take off your boxers," she pleaded, needing him inside of her.

Within seconds they were both naked, their bodies aching to connect as one. With a sigh, he gripped her shoulders. "Ciara?"

She eyed him. "What is it? Your shoulder?"

"It's fine, but are you sure about this?"

"Absolutely."

She kissed him, a long, deep kiss she hoped would convince him he had nothing to worry about. She was a big girl and knew what she wanted.

She wanted Griff.

He gripped her hips, as if wanting to be gentle and not hurt her. But Ciara couldn't stand being teased to the brink of insanity.

"I need you inside of me."

"Hang on." He ripped the foil package with his teeth and slid the condom in place.

He stroked her jaw line with his thumb. "There's no place I'd rather be than inside you, my love."

The endearment filled her soul with hope for the future. With gentle hands to her hips, he filled her with his love and she arched to greet him.

It was amazing, her complete lack of self-consciousness, his gentleness...his confession.

He'd called her his *love*.

Yes, that was the word for it and she was determined to hang on to it for the rest of her life.

GRIFF awakened a few hours later, guilt settling deep in his chest. He'd done stupid things in his life. This one was not only stupid, but it was cruel. He could only explain it as temporary insanity or pity for a woman who'd have to start all over in a few days.

Hell, it's not like he hadn't done this before, hadn't slept with a mark in order to keep things moving in the right direction.

Yeah, bud, and what direction is that? Dishonorable discharge? Supreme bastard?

What he'd done was dishonorable, all right. He'd made love to a woman he knew damn well would expect more from him. She'd expect a future with him.

Couldn't happen. He rolled out of bed, put on his shorts and glanced at his lover. Flaming-red hair with brown streaks fanned across the pillow, sheets were strewn across her hips, exposing smooth, beautiful skin and perfectly shaped breasts. Breasts he ached to taste again.

Instead he pulled the covers across her and went to the corner chair. He watched her, this beauty who'd claimed his heart. So damn fragile, so innocent. And she had so much to live for, while Griff had nothing but the pledge he'd made to a dead sister.

That's not honoring her memory, that's making her a martyr.

Ciara's words haunted him as he glanced out the window, searching the heavens for a sign from Beth. Was Ciara right? Had he been destroying himself with grief this whole time, while thinking he was honoring his sister's death?

"Beth," he whispered. "What do I do?"

His phone vibrated on the nightstand. He grabbed it and went into the hallway. "Black."

"I've got the chip," Keen said.

"So it's over."

"Not quite. Someone's taken out a hit on your girl."

Chapter Fourteen

Griff squeezed the phone, panic filling his chest. "What purpose could they have to kill her? She doesn't know anything about their business."

"You sure about that?"

"Meaning what?" Griff said.

"She knows something, something worth killing for. Whether she realizes it or not, she's a part of this."

"She didn't even know about the smuggling."

"Yet it was happening right under her nose. She probably saw an interaction or heard a conversation and even though she hasn't made sense of it, they can't risk her staying alive long enough to figure it out." Dalton said. "Looks like Granny smuggled goods but she died before the microchips were scheduled for delivery, and Lucinda Brooks is clean."

"Damn, we have to identify who's giving the orders," Griff said.

"You and the girl work on connections. Even in the program we can't guarantee they won't find her, unless she never leaves her house or has plastic surgery."

Dalton was right. WD was a great program, but even great programs could be compromised when enough money was thrown at an assassin to track down and kill a witness.

Which meant Griff would not only have to find whoever ordered the hit, but he'd also have to kill the assassin before he fulfilled his contract.

"If you need help tracking records, e-mails, anything, call my brother, Nate. He's brilliant and faster than AW techies. His number is on the fridge."

"Ciara and I will narrow down the list and call him if we need help."

"I'm handing the chips over tomorrow morning to an agent CO Andrews dispatched a few hours ago. I'll stay at my brother's in Seattle tonight, so you'll have the house to yourself."

"Thanks."

"Behave."

If the kid only knew how much Griff had misbehaved in the last few hours.

Griff turned to find Ciara coming out of the bedroom, clutching a green blanket around her shoulders.

"Hey, you're awake." He hugged her, holding on a few seconds longer than necessary. She must have sensed his concern.

"What's going on?" she said.

When she studied him like that it was hard to lie, but he didn't want to worry her. "Keen recovered the chip, but we need to work on that short list of smuggling suspects. Get dressed and meet me downstairs."

"No fair." She winked and eyed his boxers.

"Right, guess I should put something on, too." He followed her in the bedroom, slipped on his jeans and swiped his shirt from the floor. "I'll meet you downstairs."

"Then you'll tell me what's really going on?"

"Excuse me?"

"Something's put that frown between those gorgeous blue eyes of yours."

"Low blood sugar," he offered.

"Uh-huh." As if modest about Griff seeing her naked, she gently pushed him into the hall and shut the bedroom door.

He went downstairs, trying to figure out how he was going to keep her safe from a trained killer. First, they'd have to figure out what she knew that was so damned important.

He opened Dalton's laptop in the kitchen and powered up. There had to be something they'd missed, something obvious.

He slipped on his shirt and searched for coffee. They'd be up all night if necessary to figure out where the threat was coming from. He needed to put an end to this, damn it. He wanted to get her into the program where he could be sure she'd live a safe and happy life.

Splaying his hands on the counter, he leaned forward and took a deep breath, realizing Ciara's life, her happiness had taken priority over his mission. Which was exactly why falling in love was not an option in his business.

Love? Yep. He admitted to himself that that's exactly what was happening to him. He was falling, hard and fast, and there wasn't a damn thing he could do about it.

Except protect the woman he loved, today and for the rest of her life.

CIARA hesitated in the doorway concerned that Griff was so still as he leaned into the kitchen counter. He seemed lost and devastated.

Even with the gunshot wound and racing from their enemies he hadn't looked this broken.

"Griff? I've got your sling." She slipped it over his head and adjusted his arm at the proper angle. She caught his gaze and froze at the regret tinting his blue eyes.

"What is it?"

"Nothing, everything's fine."

He pulled away and opened the refrigerator. "I'm making sandwiches. Turkey okay?"

"No."

"What do you have a taste for?" he said.

"The truth."

He pulled bread from the top of the refrigerator. "Ah, the truth, that elusive thing that always messes me up."

"Just say it." She stroked his arm.

He leveled her with cold, dark eyes. "You, me, what we did upstairs, it's destroyed my focus. The mission was to recover the microchips and figure out who's been smuggling. Dalton's got half of that covered, and I need to complete the other half."

She struggled not to let his words hurt her. He was probably distancing himself because he needed to finish his mission and protect her.

"How can I help?" she said.

"Stop touching me for starters."

She snatched her hand away. It felt like he'd plunged a knife through her heart. She sensed love was not something he knew how to process.

"Okay." She dropped her hand to her side and eyed him. "Then what?"

"I'll fix sandwiches. Check your museum account e-mail. See if anything's happened since we've been gone that looks suspicious."

She sat at the computer but couldn't sign on.

"It's not recognizing my password." She glanced at him. "How can that be?"

"They've already gotten to it, wiped it out."

"I could call my computer guy and see if he knows how to—"

"We don't have background on him yet. How do you know you can trust him?"

"Pete? Oh, come on."

"You're too trusting."

She wondered if that was meant to be a warning.

"You have a better idea?" she shot back.

"Finish making sandwiches. I'll call Dalton's brother."

"You sure you can trust *him?*" she snapped.

He ignored her and made the call, ambling into the living area. She made the sandwiches, frustrated that their relationship had gone from warm and loving to cool and argumentative in less than thirty seconds.

Had their lovemaking been a diversion, something to pass the time while they waited on good news from Dalton about finding the chip?

Yet he did find the chip and Griff didn't seem all that happy. He seemed frustrated. With Ciara. What, like she was keeping something from him? Intentionally distracting his focus? Did he still suspect she was involved?

No, he wouldn't suspect her and sleep with her, would he?

Sure, isn't that what spies did?

She closed her eyes, fearing this was all a game. She wouldn't go there. She couldn't. She'd given her heart completely to this man and she couldn't stand having it broken into pieces. Wasn't losing her life as she knew it, her faith in Gran been enough loss for one week?

"Dalton's brother thinks he's got us into the archived files. Your computer programmer set up a secret archive, did you know that?"

"No."

"Put him on the suspect list."

"I can't see Pete as a criminal."

"You're a civilian, you can't see anything."

His words belittled her, made her feel stupid and ashamed. Ashamed that she'd been so gullible to think Griff actually felt something for her. Ashamed to think she was tough enough to survive this ordeal.

"Excuse me," she said, and went upstairs. She shut the bedroom door and locked it. Okay, not a mature thing to do, but she needed to get her wits about her and figure out how to ignore the pain long enough to get through this.

Heck, why should she be any different than her mom, who'd had her heart broken after fifteen years of marriage? At least Ciara's heart hadn't been crushed after years of commitment. Yet it felt like years. She realized she'd never felt this way for Thom. She'd settled for what she thought was a nice man, a safe man.

This time around she'd picked the exact opposite. But no, she didn't pick Griff. Fate had picked him for her. Well she was tired of fate making choices about her life, tired of feeling like a victim: a victim of her parents' divorce, a victim of Gran's criminal ways.

She had the power to let go of this old garbage and move forward. Give up her resentments about her up-bringing, give up her fear of her current situation and even her anger with Griff. She accepted her situation and welcomed the chance to be put into the witness program and start a new life. How many women got the chance to do that, right? Only, in this new life, she'd set her own goals, disregard the needs of others and lock her heart in a place where no one could touch it.

THEY'D spent the entire night going through computer files, Ciara pointing out anything that didn't seem right.

She seemed like a stranger, Griff thought. Gone was the sweet, caring woman who'd found bliss in his arms. Gone was the hopeful, optimistic tone of her voice, the sparkle in her green eyes.

He'd done that to her. He'd destroyed her innocence with his darkness.

It would have happened sooner or later.

"This is too frustrating." She stood and paced to the coffeepot. "And this coffee is useless." She shoved her mug to the counter. "It's not helping me think straight at all."

"Things are always the most frustrating before a breakthrough. Come back and go through these last files with me."

She planted her hands to her hips and for a second he thought she'd defy him. He almost said please, but couldn't risk being nice to her. Keeping his emotional distance, keeping her angry with him was the only way to guarantee her safety.

She needed to embrace the witness program and abandon her old life...and Griff.

As she ran her finger down the list of folders on her work's server, Griff swallowed hard at the memory of the way those gentle fingers touched him, lit his skin with need.

He stood and got coffee, no cream this time, something to shock him out of his thoughts. He was drifting because he lacked sleep, that's all.

Probably wouldn't get any sleep for a while. He couldn't risk falling asleep knowing a predator was out there, hunting Ciara.

"What is this?" she said.

He leaned forward and studied the screen, struggling to ignore her sweet scent. "What?"

"I didn't send this e-mail."

He read the e-mail dated yesterday from the doll-museum account to blackdeath@lucifer.com.

Destroy the red-haired, fairy doll. Immediately.

"We'd never destroy merchandise. That's crazy."

Griff knew the meaning of the e-mail. Ciara was the doll, which meant the hit originated from the doll museum. "Go on to bed," Griff said. "A little sleep might help us think straight."

He closed the program, acting as if he was going to bed, as well.

"Sorry," she said.

From the tone in her voice she thought Griff was upset with her, not with this frustrating case.

As she walked toward the stairs, he stood in the kitchen doorway, wanting to call her back to apologize for being an ass. He ached to explain that what was driving him mad was the thought of her being killed.

The thought of never hearing her voice again or touching her amazingly soft skin again.

He leaned into the doorjamb and listened to her climb the stairs, go into the guest room and shut the door.

Truth was, after tomorrow he never *would* touch her again or kiss her again, not if he wanted to keep her alive.

"I'm sorry, sweetheart," he whispered.

Then he went to work. He signed on to the computer and wrote an e-mail using her personal e-mail address.

I'm concerned about an e-mail requesting destruction of a Tonner doll. I'll be back in town tomorrow night. Whoever sent this request please meet me at the museum at 7 p.m. —Ciara

He hit Send and went for another cup of coffee. Whether the person behind the hit answered or not, Griff could be pretty sure the message would be given to the assassin, who'd show up tomorrow to finish his job.

Griff would be there to eliminate the bastard before he got close to Ciara.

He checked the kitchen clock. Three-thirty. Dalton should be back by noon to watch Ciara. Griff didn't want to leave her alone and vulnerable with no one to protect her.

Yet she'd have to get used to being alone in the program. But not for long. Ciara would make friends in days. He figured it would take all of a few months for her to attract a man into her life. Griff suddenly knew he'd have to keep track of where they placed her. He wasn't going to let her get seriously involved with any man until he did a complete background check.

Even if Griff couldn't have her in his life, he'd make sure no one would hurt or deceive her in her new life. He'd be her guardian angel, her protector.

He'd do the one thing for Ciara he couldn't do for his own sister. He'd keep her safe for the rest of her life.

Chapter Fifteen

Ciara awakened and fought back a wave of sadness. Griff hadn't joined her in bed. Of course not. He was done with her.

It would be over soon, she reminded herself. Griff would pass her to the people in the witness protection program, and she'd start her new life. Alone.

How did she let herself be fooled by his kisses, by his touch? Fooled into thinking he loved her?

Silly girl. People didn't fall in love so quickly, the rational side of her brain scolded.

Her heart spoke otherwise. She had fallen in love. It wasn't some kind of syndrome or mental illness. It was a true connection to a part of her she'd kept hidden since her parents' divorce. Too bad the connection had been wasted on a cold bastard like Griff.

She dressed in jeans and a T-shirt and went downstairs, repeating affirmations in her head: *I'm an independent woman, and I don't need Griff.*

She spotted Dalton Keen sprawled on the living room sofa. He'd made it back safely, which was good. The microchip threat must be over.

In search of coffee, she spotted an envelope with her

name on it on the kitchen counter. She opened it and found some cash. Her heart sunk even lower, if that was possible.

Dalton stumbled into the kitchen. "You're awake," he said, reaching for coffee.

"Where is he?" She felt like a whore and wanted to slap Griff across that handsome face of his.

"Left a few hours ago."

"Bastard," she said.

"Hey, ya' know, I never did like your attitude, but that was completely uncalled for." He poured a cup of coffee.

"Okay, how about coward?"

"Lady, you have no idea what you're talking about."

"Sure I do. He ran away because looking at me reminded him that he's lost his integrity."

"Whatever." He went to his computer and logged in.

"I have feelings for Griff and he had something to do with that. He slept with me, damn it." Her voice cracked.

Dalton's fingers froze on the keyboard. "He shouldn't have done that."

"No kidding. Is that part of the game with you guys? Sleep with as many women as possible and keep score?"

He stood so fast she backed up. "You have no idea what it's like to do what we do."

"Thank God for that."

"Some of us might be bastards, sure, but not Griff. He saved my life, and now he's out to save yours."

"By making me fall in love with him and breaking my heart, then abandoning me without even saying bye?"

"By going after your killer."

"Excuse me?"

"There's a hit on you. Griff's gone after the assassin. A man doesn't risk his job, hell, his *life* for someone he doesn't care about, so zip it."

She clutched the coffee mug and tried to puzzle through Dalton's words. Griff was risking everything for her? But last night he'd acted like their relationship was a one-night stand.

After their lovemaking she remembered the mysterious call and how different he acted when she came downstairs. Was that the call informing him about the assassin?

He'd probably been rude, even cruel to push her away so he could get his focus back. So he could save her life by killing the assassin before he found her.

Her instincts had been right on. Griff loved her.

"He left you money because from this point on you can't access your bank accounts, talk to anyone in your past or do anything relating to Ciara O'Malley." Dalton pulled his cell phone from his pocket. "I've got to take this. The plan is I'll escort you to Portland after I get word from Griff that the assassin has been taken out. Should be later tonight."

He paced into the living room, leaving Ciara alone in the kitchen.

Griff had left her money, not as payment for sex, but to help her get started in her new life. He'd put her needs before his mission and he'd put his life in direct danger for her, not because she was an assignment, but because he loved her.

She collapsed at the computer and stared at the screen, still open from last night's investigative work. She noticed someone had sent an e-mail from her personal account. She signed on and spotted an unopened e-mail received a few hours ago.

Will wait for you in the furnace room.

Below it, she noticed an e-mail sent early this morning

about her returning to the museum to speak to whoever sent the e-mail about destroying dolls. Ciara didn't send it, which meant Griff sent it to draw out the assassin.

Will wait for you in the furnace room.

Adele's words rushed back:

If you don't replace that thing soon, it's going to blow up the entire block.

It dawned on her that the assassin was going to blow up the museum, figuring Ciara would be caught in the blast and killed. Made sense. No one would suspect a professional hit if Ciara died thanks to a faulty furnace.

She had to reach Griff, tell him not to go inside the museum. Grabbing the house phone she realized she didn't have his number. She raced into the living room and tapped Dalton on the shoulder.

"I need to talk to Griff."

He ignored her.

"Now!"

Dalton eyed her. "Kid, let me call you back." He ended his call and glared at her. "What's the problem?"

"It's a set up. There was an e-mail telling him to go to the furnace room, but it's an old furnace and it's going to blow up."

"How can you possibly know that?"

"Call him, I need to warn him."

He punched in Griff's number and handed her the phone.

It rang three times and went into voicemail. She closed her eyes at the sound of his voice.

She handed the phone to Dalton. "He's not answering. Why isn't he answering?"

"He's probably in a dead zone or something. He'll be fine. Go get something to eat. I brought home doughnuts."

"But—"

"I need to call my brother back. Go on." He pointed toward the kitchen.

His brother. The guy was chatting with family while Griff was walking into a trap at the museum. Dalton didn't take her seriously, didn't think she knew what she was talking about.

He turned his back to her and went to the front door. "Sorry," he said into the phone. "Female issues. Yeah, right." He chuckled and shut the door behind him.

Dalton thought she was an ignorant girl, panicking over nothing. But it wasn't nothing. It was Griff's life. She wouldn't let him be killed trying to protect her. She scanned the room and her eyes caught on Dalton's car keys sitting on the counter. She spotted his truck out back. She snatched the keys, ripped the cash from the envelope Griff had left her and grabbed a few doughnuts for the road. She'd leave her things behind, her purse, clothes and her fear.

Griff was walking into a trap for her because he loved her. She wouldn't let him die. She went to the front window and eyed Dalton, deep in conversation with his brother. She quietly locked the front door to give herself time make her escape and get to Griff.

With newfound determination, she went out the back door, got into Dalton's SUV and took off, sighing with relief when she didn't see him chasing after her. Good, she'd make the Bainbridge ferry this afternoon and get to the museum before Griff lost his life. For her.

She realized putting someone's life before one's own was the ultimate sacrifice of love. Now it was her turn, one last time, to be the protector. She'd save Griff and challenge him to explore their relationship in a new place with new names and clean slate. They'd both survive the assassin's plan and live out their lives in each other's arms.

Armed with the power of love and renewed determination, she headed for the ferry.

"CALM DOWN, kid. You're getting way ahead of yourself," Dalton said to his little brother, Nate.

"No, no, listen to me. Something about that chip looked familiar, and I did some digging."

Dalton tensed. "Nate, I told you I didn't want you involved in this. I showed it to you for feedback, that's all. Hell, if my boss found out I showed it to a civilian I'd be——"

"I've seen it before."

"Of course you did. They all look the same."

"Not this one. Wait, someone's beeping in. It might be Pete. I sent him the specs, and he was going to——"

"Damn it, you told someone else about this?"

"Hang on."

The line went silent and Dalton scolded himself for involving his brother in this assignment. But the kid was a computer genius and if anyone could figure out if the chip was the right one and not a dummy, it was Nathaniel Keen.

Dalton cursed his brother's curiosity, his curiosity and need to impress Dalton. It had always been that way, Dalton excelling in sports, while Nate was at home taking apart the TV. The kid had been sick as a child and found comfort in books. As he'd outgrown his illness his maturity seemed a bit stunted, but his intelligence soared. And at twenty-three he'd landed himself a top IT job at a major corporation in Seattle. He was a success, yet always struggled to feel as important as his soldier brother.

Dalton went to the front door. It was locked.

"What the hell?" He tapped on the door, peering into the house, but the girl was nowhere. Was she sulking upstairs because she couldn't talk to Griff? She'd made up a cockamamie excuse to call him wanting to warn him about a faulty furnace. How had she dreamed up that one?

"Open up!" he ordered, pounding on the door.

A park maintenance worker drove by and slowed. Dalton waved and stopped pounding.

Between the bossy girl and his dramatic brother, he was going to lose his mind. He went around to the back door. The truck was gone.

"What the hell?" He hung up on his brother and knocked on the back door. She stole his truck? He was a complete failure by letting her get away. Hell, she might as well pin a bull's-eye to her chest.

His cell vibrated and the ID read Nathaniel Keen.

"I've got an emergency, Nate. I can't talk."

"But you're not going to believe what Pistol Pete said about the chip."

"Pistol Pete? How old is he, fourteen? I've got a work emergency. Forget about the chip, kid. That's an order. I'll call you later."

He hung up and cursed himself for involving Nate in this at all, but Dalton needed to move this case along to gain favor with his CO and it was obvious Griff wasn't thinking with his brains.

Dalton eyed the empty driveway. Talk about brainless. He couldn't even call the doc to borrow his car because he'd already loaned it to Griff for his trip into the city. They figured terrorist agents might have spotted Dalton's car at the UPS warehouse. If that was the case, they didn't want Griff being noticed in Dalton's car when he got to the museum.

No wheels. No Ciara. Time for Dalton to punt.

THE FERRY gods had been on Ciara's side. She made it to Seattle by five-thirty and to the museum by six, making sure to drive just under the speed limit. The last thing she needed was to be pulled over in a stolen truck with no license. She pulled off 405 and headed to the museum. She parked on the street not wanting to be obvious. It was Sunday and the museum was closed, which meant there'd be no cars in the lot.

Yet a white Mercedes was parked just outside the door. Lucinda's car? What was she doing here? Was she the one who orchestrated this and showed up to lure Ciara inside where the assassin was waiting?

Lucinda didn't get out of her car.

Ciara felt helpless. What did she think she was going to do when she showed up? Find Griff, that's what. But how? The window to the furnace room. She'd sneak over there and call inside, hoping he was already in place, waiting for the assassin.

A second car pulled up. A Ford Taurus.

"Oh, no."

Adele got out and led Lucinda into the museum.

Ciara opened her door and tried to call out, but her voice caught in her throat. She had to stop Lucinda from hurting Adele.

Ciara raced across the street to the museum door and punched the code, but the door didn't open. Strange. Someone had changed the code?

Then she realized how exposed she was. She jumped between the bushes and the building and edged her way to the furnace-room window. She kneeled in the soft earth and tapped on the window, then searched for something hard to break the glass.

"I knew you'd come back."

She froze at the sound of the familiar male voice. It was the dirty cop, Officer Banks. Was he the assassin?

She put up her hands.

"Put your hands down." He pulled her to her feet. "Come join your friend." He shoved her toward the entrance to the museum. "Where's your boyfriend, huh? My partner would love to get a piece of him after he gets out of the hospital."

Officer Banks punched in a code and the front door opened.

"Got her," he called out. The door locked with a deafening click behind her.

Griff, where are you? She wanted to look into those blue eyes one more time, tell him she loved him, tell him she understood.

From around the corner came the shooter from Whidbey Island, the man she'd run off the cliff.

"You look like you've seen a ghost," he taunted. "I don't die that easy. This way." He motioned with his gun.

She headed for the furnace room. As they passed the break room Ciara spotted Adele and Lucinda sitting at the table.

"We've got her," the assassin said to Lucinda.

Banks motioned for the women to join Ciara in the hallway.

"Adele, I'm so sorry," Ciara said.

She walked beside Lucinda. "You should be. Everything was running so smoothly until you ran off with that government agent."

"Excuse me?"

"Take them downstairs," Adele ordered.

"What? *Adele,*" Ciara hushed, disbelief stabbing her in the heart.

"You were always so naive and trusting," Adele said, following them. "More so than your grandmother. She figured it out in the end, which is why she had to die."

"What!" Ciara lunged at Adele, but Banks restrained her.

"And now you will join Ruthie up in heaven." Adele smiled, eyeing Lucinda. "I've set up Missy Lucinda here to take the blame, along with you and your grandmother. See, your grandmother was a smuggler for years and when she passed, you took over. You and Lucinda had quite the business going. But alas, you died when the furnace blew up. 'Officer, I warned Ciara to replace that old furnace,'" she acted. "The official story is faulty equipment, but the government will know the truth. They'll suspect you were set up to die because you failed to deliver the microchips."

"It's been you all along?"

"Yes, it's been my keeping track of you through my concerned phone calls, my keeping the business going. You should have stayed out of it, but no, you decided to take over and screw things up. And I still don't have the merchandise. Where is it?"

Ciara just shook her head. "Adele, why are you doing this?"

"I'm taking control of my life. Roger left me with nothing. I have to beg my ungrateful daughter for money. Do you know how that feels? To be abandoned?"

"Actually, I do."

"Oh, sure, you with your loving grandmother. Stupid woman, she convinced herself we were importing specialties for collectors. She started a fund for you, her precious granddaughter and donated the rest to Women in Trouble. How ridiculous is that? She saved nothing for herself. She would have been broke and alone with no one to take care of her."

"I would have always been there for her."

"Bull. A man like Mr. Blue Eyes would have swept you off your feet, you naive, ignorant girl. Ruth was ignorant until the end, when she discovered my plan to smuggle in the chips."

"Adele, those chips will kill people. Your family travels. What if your granddaughter was on a plane and it crashed because of you?"

Adele slapped Ciara and she fell to her knees. Lucinda cried out.

"Shut up or I'll hit you, too." Adele glared at Ciara. "I've been wanting to do that. You spoiled, selfish brat."

Okay, the woman was insane. Ciara could be called many things, but spoiled wasn't one of them. Ciara stood.

"Why?"

"Money is power."

"But why hire an assassin to kill me?"

"To draw out your lover. Speaking of which, where is he?"

"I don't know."

Adele slapped her again. This time Ciara did not go down.

"Where?"

Ciara rubbed her cheek. "He left early this morning. They have the chips. He doesn't care what happens to me."

Adele laughed, a high-pitched sinister sound, then suddenly it stopped as if someone flipped a switch. "Take them to the furnace room."

Officer Banks yanked Ciara down the hall. The Whidbey Island shooter dragged Lucinda and she tripped.

"Take the damn shoes off," the shooter said. "You're not going to need them."

Lucinda whimpered and slipped off her high heels. They led Ciara and Lucinda down into the furnace room.

"Need to be sure you don't squirm out of this one," Banks said, binding Ciara's wrists with flexi-cuffs to a shelving unit.

As he bound Lucinda's wrists Ciara caught sight of Griff's blue eyes watching her from behind the furnace. She snapped her gaze to the shooter, just as he knocked Banks out with the butt of his gun.

"Officer Banks will be joining you today, girls," the shooter said. "Have a nice trip."

As he turned to leave, Griff charged the guy and they both went down, slamming against the cement floor. Griff pistol-whipped the shooter with the butt of his gun, knocking him unconscious.

He glared over his shoulder at Ciara. "What the hell are you doing here?"

"I had to warn you about the furnace. It's going to blow. Adele is the bad guy, we need to get out of here!" Ciara struggled to get up.

Griff started up the stairs, but Adele loomed in the doorway.

"You all need to die!" She fired the gun, missing Griff, who jumped off the stairs and took cover behind a storage unit.

Adele fired off three more rounds and slammed the door.

He went to the furnace and analyzed the device. "Is there another way out of here?"

"Window?" Ciara said. "It's kind of small, but…how long have we got?"

"Fifteen minutes."

Lucinda whimpered.

Griffin pulled a knife from his boot and cut the flexi-cuffs off Ciara.

"Why didn't you answer your phone?" she said.

"No signal down here." He cut off Lucinda's cuffs.

"Why didn't you tell me about the assassin?" Ciara pushed.

"Can we do this later? Up you go." He hoisted Lucinda up and through the window. "Your turn."

He grabbed Ciara by the waist, and she kissed him.

Sure, Griff loved the taste of her, but right now this distraction could end both their lives.

He broke the kiss. "I'll take a rain check. When you get outside run as far away from the building as possible."

He gently pushed her through the window and she turned to him, as if needing to say something.

"Take my cell and call Dalton for help," he said, wanting to avoid an emotional moment. "He'll know what to do."

"Aren't you coming?"

"I'll never fit through the window, sweetheart. I'll find another way."

"I'm not leaving you."

"Please, for once trust that I know what I'm doing. I swear if you die, I might as well be dead. Get the hell out of here and give me the peace of mind that you're going to be okay. Please?" He squeezed her hand. "I'll figure out a way to get to you, I promise."

His heart pounded against his chest in sync with the ticking of the timer behind him. He was down to nine, maybe eight minutes before the place blew.

"You'd better find me or I'll never forgive you."

"Go," he ordered.

She kissed his hand, grabbed Lucinda and ran.

Ciara pressed the speed dial for Dalton Keen and raced for safety. Griff was a pro, he'd know how to get out of there before the place went up in flames. He'd asked her to trust him and she would.

She heard gunfire, and she and Lucinda raced around the corner of the building next door.

Ciara glanced at the museum. "She's not shooting at us. She's trying to keep Griff in the basement. I've got to help him. Here." She handed Lucinda the phone. "Talk to this guy and tell him where we are and what's happening. I'm going to draw Adele away from the furnace room so Griff can get out."

Ciara sprinted across the parking lot and grabbed the clay flowerpot overflowing with pansies and tossed it through the glass door.

"I'm out here!" Ciara called, then hid behind a rhododendron bush.

"Those idiots! How did you get out?" Adele raced outside.

Ciara took a deep breath and tackled the woman, knocking her to the ground.

"Nice move," Dalton said, coming up beside her.

"How did you get here so quick?" she said, then shook her head. "It's going to blow."

"Get around the corner with your friend."

"No, Griff's inside, I have to—"

"Good God, woman, all he wants is for you to be safe. Don't screw that up now by walking into an explosion. Come on."

They went to the safe spot beside Lucinda, Dalton carrying Adele over his shoulder.

Come on, Griff. "Where is he?" she asked Dalton. An explosion rocked the ground and she gripped her jacket above her chest. "He's okay. Griff's okay," she whispered. He had to be.

Dalton put his phone to his ear. "I've got them, sir. There are three of them."

"The old lady is the smuggler," Ciara absently offered. "Lucinda is an innocent bystander."

Dalton eyed Lucinda. "We've identified the smuggler and there's an innocent. I think she's in shock. No, sir, no sign of him."

Ciara closed her eyes. She couldn't breathe past the pain.

"Yes, sir." Dalton strained to look over his shoulder. "I see it."

A black suburban with tinted windows pulled up. "And we're off," he whispered. Dalton bound Adele's wrists and shoved her into the back.

He turned to Lucinda. "Come on, we'll get you help." He pulled her up and handed her off to an agent in the backseat of the truck.

"Let's go, Ciara, before the cops show up."

"I can't go without Griff."

Dalton kneeled beside her and tipped her chin to look at him. "You've come this far. Don't let him down."

"But if I leave him—"

"Do you love him?"

She snapped her gaze to his hazel eyes. "Yes."

"Then he'll always be with you."

And that's when she knew that Dalton Keen also thought Griff had died in the blast.

Chapter Sixteen

Motions. Ciara went through the motions of a twenty-nine-year-old woman, yet she might as well be a zombie. She'd lost half of her heart the day Griff disappeared. She'd heard the news reports. The bodies of two men were found in the museum, which meant either one of the bad guys had escaped or Griff had.

Which was worse, she wondered? Griff dying in the blast or abandoning her on purpose?

It didn't matter. The end result was the same. She felt hollow inside.

She wandered the beach, tempted to walk into the waves and drown her sorrows and her soul in the cool waters of Lake Michigan. She'd entered the program and was now an innkeeper for Holland House, a B and B in Michigan. She'd been at it for a month now, faking a bright smile for travelers, kneading dough for scones and bread, making coffee in the morning and putting chocolates on pillows at night.

She always was good at taking care of everyone else. She wished Griff were around so she could take care of him.

Would she ever know the truth about what happened

to him? She'd tried getting more out of Dalton Keen, but he wasn't talking. He probably blamed her for Griff's death. Why not? She did.

Oh, she was a sad Sally. What happened to her plans to start a new life with hope and passion and excitement?

"Don't be so hard on yourself," she whispered. She needed to recover from the shock of losing Griff and finding out Adele was a smuggler who'd killed Gran.

Nothing is what it appears to be, she thought, then glanced up and spotted a mirage of Griff, walking along the shore.

She'd seen that one before. As soon as he got close his face would change into that of a stranger.

Maybe she should see a shrink. Couldn't hurt, right? It could help her process the loss of Griff, a man she shouldn't technically have fallen in love with in the short time they had together.

She wandered back to the inn, feeling a little better after her walk. It had been weeks since she'd gone far from her new home and she wondered if deep down she still feared for her life. No, it wasn't that. It was a lack of energy, energy drained by grief.

She climbed the stairs to the kitchen and inhaled the wonderful aroma of fresh-baked bread.

"Hey, Maria," she greeted.

Maria was a forty-something, nurturing woman. Some days Ciara wondered if she was an agent assigned to keep an eye on her.

"Hey, that was on my schedule for this afternoon," Ciara said.

"I don't mind. Besides, you've got an obnoxious customer to deal with upstairs." She aimed the rolling pin at the ceiling.

"I didn't have anyone scheduled to check in today." She went to her book and scanned the week. "Nope."

"A drop-in named Nicholas Drake. I didn't think you'd mind since we're empty. Then he started complaining about this and that. If I would have known I would have said, 'No Vacancy.'"

"Don't suppose I can hide?" Ciara said. She really didn't have the energy to mollify a guest.

"I told him I'd send up the manager when you got back. He's in the Coastal View room."

"Has he got fresh towels?"

"Yes."

"Chocolate?"

"He wasn't nice enough for chocolate." Maria winked.

Ciara grabbed a fancy china plate and placed some truffles in the center. "Never hurts to bring a bribe."

"Good luck with that."

Ciara climbed the stairs and tried to keep a positive attitude. It wouldn't take much to make her cry today. But she needed to be professional, swallow her sadness and paste on the cheery innkeeper face, at least long enough to pacify her disgruntled guest.

She hesitated outside the Coastal View room. The door was cracked open. She took a deep breath and knocked. "Mr. Drake?"

"Come," a male voice said from inside the bathroom.

She stepped inside and froze at the sight of flower bouquets filling the room.

"Are you expecting company?" she asked.

"Just you." And out of the bathroom stepped a blond Griffin Black.

Joy rushed to her cheeks and filled her heart.

"Whoa, sweetheart, don't fall down on me." Griff

steadied her with an arm to her waist. He guided her to sit on the bed.

"You're blond," she said, stupidly.

He eyed the chocolates. "For me?"

"Yes." She gripped the plate as if holding on to a building ledge for dear life.

"These are all for you." He motioned to the colorful arrangements.

Ciara didn't take her eyes off of the clearest, most brilliant shade of blue. Griff's eyes. He was alive, here, with her.

"I'm mad at you," she said.

"I'm sorry."

"I thought you were dead, or maybe not dead, but then you left me, and no one would talk to me and Dalton Keen is a jerk, and—"

"Shh." He pressed his forefinger to her lips and grabbed the plate with his other hand.

But she wouldn't give it up. Wouldn't let him take one more thing from her.

"Okay, maybe you need to hold on to that."

"You lied to me." A tear slipped down her cheek.

"Ciara, you have to understand something. My life is hell if you aren't safe. I had some things to work out to make sure I wouldn't put you in danger by being with you. Can you understand that?"

"No."

"I've resigned my post, Ciara, taken an indefinite leave in order to be with you."

"But…you quit?"

"I'm on leave until I figure out what else I can do for the U.S. government."

"I thought that your job is what you lived for."

"It was. Until I met you." He brushed a strand of hair off her cheek. "You were right, honey. I wasn't honoring Beth's memory. I was sullying it. She would want me to live and love."

"Are you going away again?"

"Not unless you send me away."

"Why would I do that?"

"Because you're angry with me."

"I'm furious."

"I know." He studied the chocolates on the plate. "But it was the safest way to start over. For both of us."

"Griff—"

"Nicholas, actually. My name is Nicholas Drake." He smiled. "I believe this is yours." He pulled her Tinkerbell necklace from his pocket. "Just like Tinkerbell needs people to believe in her to live, I was hoping you could believe, you know, in us."

She slid the plate onto the nightstand. Her love was here in her home and he'd filled this special room with flowers. He was, in his way, asking for forgiveness.

She shook his hand. "Nice to meet you, Nicholas Drake. My name is Tina Edwards."

"Miss Edwards," he said. "Mind if a stay a while in your fine establishment?"

"You, sir, may stay as long as you like."

She leaned forward and kissed Griff knowing this would be the first of many nights they'd spend in each other's arms.

* * * * *

Next month, Assignment: The Girl Next Door *concludes with* RENEGADE SOLDIER, *only from Pat White and Harlequin Intrigue!*

Harlequin is 60 years old, and Harlequin Blaze is celebrating!
After all, a lot can happen in 60 years, or 60 minutes...or 60 seconds!
Find out what's going down in Blaze's heart-stopping new mini-series,
FROM 0 TO 60!
Getting from "Hello" to "How was it?" can happen fast....

Here's a sneak peek of the first book,
A LONG, HARD RIDE
by Alison Kent
Available March 2009

"Is that for me?" Trey asked.

Cardin Worth cocked her head to the side and considered how much better the day already seemed. "Good morning to you, too."

When she didn't hold out the second cup of coffee for him to take, he came closer. She sipped from her heavy white mug, hiding her grin and her giddy rush of nerves behind it.

But when he stopped in front of her, she made the mistake of lowering her gaze from his face to the exposed strip of his chest. It was either give him his cup of coffee or bury her nose against him and breathe in. She remembered so clearly how he smelled. How he tasted.

She gave him his coffee.

After taking a quick gulp, he smiled and said, "Good morning, Cardin. I hope the floor wasn't too hard for you."

The hardness of the floor hadn't been the problem. She shook her head. "Are you kidding? I slept like a baby, swaddled in my sleeping bag."

"In my sleeping bag, you mean."

If he wanted to get technical, yeah. "Thanks for the

loaner. It made sleeping on the floor almost bearable."
As had the warmth of his spooned body, she thought,
then quickly changed the subject. "I saw you have a loaf
of bread and some eggs. Would you like me to cook
breakfast?"

He lowered his coffee mug slowly, his gaze as warm
as the sun on her shoulders, as the ceramic heating her
hands. "I didn't bring you out here to wait on me."

"You didn't bring me out here at all. I volunteered to
come."

"To help me get ready for the race. Not to serve me."

"It's just breakfast, Trey. And coffee." Even if last
night it had been more. Even if the way he was looking
at her made her want to climb back into that sleeping
bag. "I work much better when my stomach's not
growling. I thought it might be the same for you."

"It is, but I'll cook. You made the coffee."

"That's because I can't work at all without caffeine."

"If I'd known that, I would've put on a pot as soon I
got up."

"What time *did* you get up?" Judging by the sun's
position, she swore it couldn't be any later than seven
now. And, yeah, they'd agreed to start working at six.

"Maybe four?" he guessed, giving her a lazy smile.

"But it was almost two..." She let the sentence
dangle, finishing the thought privately. She was quite
sure he knew exactly what time they'd finally fallen
asleep after he'd made love to her.

The question facing her now was where did this relationship—if you could even call it *that*—go from here?

* * * * *

*Cardin and Trey are about to find out that great sex is
only the beginning....
Don't miss the fireworks!
Get ready for
A LONG, HARD RIDE
by Alison Kent
Available March 2009,
wherever Blaze books are sold.*

CELEBRATE
60 YEARS
OF PURE READING PLEASURE
WITH HARLEQUIN®!

We'll be spotlighting a different series
every month throughout 2009
to celebrate our 60th anniversary.

Look for Harlequin® Blaze™ in March!

0-60

*After all, a lot can happen in 60 years,
or 60 minutes...or 60 seconds!*

Find out what's going down in Blaze's
heart-stopping new miniseries *0-60!*
Getting from "Hello" to "How was it?"
can happen fast....

Look for the brand-new 0-60 miniseries in March 2009!

HARLEQUIN® *Romance*®

This February the Harlequin® Romance series
will feature six Diamond Brides stories featuring
diamond proposals and gorgeous grooms.

Share your dream wedding proposal and you could WIN!

The most romantic entry will win a diamond
necklace and will inspire a proposal in one of
our upcoming Diamond Grooms books in 2010.

In 100 words or less, tell us the most romantic
way that you dream of being proposed to.

For more information, and to enter
the Diamond Brides Proposal contest, please visit
www.DiamondBridesProposal.com

Or mail your entry to us at:

IN THE U.S.: 3010 Walden Ave., P.O. Box 9069, Buffalo, NY 14269-9069
IN CANADA: 225 Duncan Mill Road, Don Mills, ON M3B 3K9

REQUEST YOUR FREE BOOKS!

2 FREE NOVELS PLUS 2 FREE GIFTS!

HARLEQUIN®

INTRIGUE®

Breathtaking Romantic Suspense

You're invited to join our Tell Harlequin Reader Panel!

By joining our new reader panel you will:

- Receive Harlequin® books—they are FREE and yours to keep with no obligation to purchase anything!
- Participate in fun online surveys
- Exchange opinions and ideas with women just like you
- Have a say in our new book ideas and help us publish the best in women's fiction

In addition, you will have a chance to win great prizes and receive special gifts!
See Web site for details. Some conditions apply.
Space is limited

To join, visit us at
www.TellHarlequin.com.

Coming Next Month

Available March 10, 2009

Spring is here and romance is in the air this month
as Harlequin Romance® takes you on a whirlwind journey
to meet gorgeous grooms!

#4081 BRADY: THE REBEL RANCHER Patricia Thayer
Second in the **Texas Brotherhood** duet. Injured pilot Brady falls for the
lovely Lindsey Stafford, but she has secrets that could destroy him. Now
Brady must fight again, this time for love....

#4082 ITALIAN GROOM, PRINCESS BRIDE Rebecca Winters
We visit the **Royal House of Savoy** as Princess Regina's arranged
wedding day approaches. Royal gardener Dizo has one chance to risk
all—and claim his princess bride!

#4083 FALLING FOR HER CONVENIENT HUSBAND Jessica Steele
Successful lawyer Phelix isn't the same shy teenager Nathan
conveniently wed eight years ago. He hasn't seen her since, and her
transformation hasn't escaped the English tycoon's notice....

#4084 CINDERELLA'S WEDDING WISH Jessica Hart
In Her Shoes...
Celebrity playboy Rafe is *not* Miranda's idea of Prince Charming. But
when she's hired as his assistant, Miranda is shocked to learn that Rafe
has hidden depths.

#4085 HER CATTLEMAN BOSS Barbara Hannay
When Kate inherits half a run-down cattle station, she doesn't expect to
have a sexy cattleman boss, Noah, to contend with! As they toil under
the hot sun, romance is on the horizon....

#4086 THE ARISTOCRAT AND THE SINGLE MOM Michelle Douglas
Handsome English aristocrat Simon keeps to himself. But, thrown into
the middle of single mom Kate's lively family on a trip to Australia, Simon
finds his buttoned-up manner slowly undone.

HRCNMBPA0209